CHANCE IN CHAINS

LECTOR HOUSE PUBLIC DOMAIN WORKS

This book is a result of an effort made by Lector House towards making a contribution to the preservation and repair of original classic literature. The original text is in the public domain in the United States of America, and possibly other countries depending upon their specific copyright laws.

In an attempt to preserve, improve and recreate the original content, certain conventional norms with regard to typographical mistakes, hyphenations, punctuations and/or other related subject matters, have been corrected upon our consideration. However, few such imperfections might not have been rectified as they were inherited and preserved from the original content to maintain the authenticity and construct, relevant to the work. The work might contain a few prior copyright references as well as page references which have been retained, wherever considered relevant to the part of the construct. We believe that this work holds historical, cultural and/or intellectual importance in the literary works community, therefore despite the oddities, we accounted the work for print as a part of our continuing effort towards preservation of literary work and our contribution towards the development of the society as a whole, driven by our beliefs.

We are grateful to our readers for putting their faith in us and accepting our imperfections with regard to preservation of the historical content. We shall strive hard to meet up to the expectations to improve further to provide an enriching reading experience.

Though, we conduct extensive research in ascertaining the status of copyright before redeveloping a version of the content, in rare cases, a classic work might be incorrectly marked as not-in-copyright. In such cases, if you are the copyright holder, then kindly contact us or write to us, and we shall get back to you with an immediate course of action.

HAPPY READING!

CHANCE IN CHAINS

GUY THORNE
(CYRIL ARTHUR EDWARD RANGER GULL)

9 789356 146853
ISBN: 978-93-5614-685-3

Published: 1914

LECTOR HOUSE

LECTOR HOUSE LLP
E-MAIL: info@lectorhouse.com

IN FRONT OF BASIL GREGORY WAS A PILE OF GOLD.

CHANCE IN CHAINS

A STORY OF MONTE CARLO

BY

GUY THORNE

Author of "When it was Dark," "The Drunkard," etc.

WITH FRONTISPIECE FROM A DRAWING BY HOWARD T. GRAVES

1914

CONTENTS

PART I

CHANCE IN CHAINS

CHAPTER I

It was nine o'clock at night, and the thirty huge dynamos of the Société Générale Electrique of Paris were nearly all at work. In the great glass-roofed hall of the Mont Parnasse Central Power Station blue-bloused workmen moved quietly over the shining floors of white concrete, pausing now and then by this or that purring, spitting monster, scrutinising the whirring, glittering copper drums, listening with experienced ears for the slightest variation in the deep wasp-like hum, touching a lever here, adjusting a screw there, or oiling a bearing with tin cans beaked like a snipe.

Huge arc lamps hanging from the ceiling cast a steel-blue radiance over the hall, a radiance so cruel and intense that the shadows of the machinery which were thrown upon the floor were as black and sharply defined as fretwork of ebony.

The incandescent lamps which showed above each of the three great switchboards of brass and vulcanite, although they were burning at full power, glowed orange in the stupendous light from above.

The monster dynamos were making light for half eastern Paris. The Gare Mont Parnasse, from where trains were running every two minutes with late business folk to Meudon, Sèvres and Versailles, was lit from this room. The dinner tables of the foreign Ambassadors on the Quai Austerlitz were illuminated by favour of these serene, relentless marvels, and, across the Seine, many a glittering café upon the heights of the pleasure city Montmartre were switching on hundreds of fresh lights in the expectation of their supper custom—even as a new dynamo was started to cope with the extra strain.

At one side of the hall a few concrete steps led into the little glass-fronted room where the superintendent engineer on duty always sat.

The room was some twelve feet square, walled with white tiles like a model dairy, and from where he sat at a deal table the engineer could look out into every part of the hall. In the hall itself it was cold, though the electricians felt but little of it owing to the fresh ozone constantly liberated from the dynamos into the air. Outside, in Paris, it was bitterly cold—a damp and foggy cold of late November. But in the room of the superintendent engineer an electric stove burned brightly and warmed it.

Two people were in the room now, Emile Deschamps and Basil Gregory, both of them employed by the Société Générale.

Deschamps was a young man of about twenty-six. His jet black hair, closely cropped to a rather large and well-shaped head, together with the swarthy tint of his complexion, proclaimed him of the South, a veritable son of the Midi from Orange, Avignon, or Marseilles. He wore a small black moustache, and his long-fingered right hand was deeply stained with the juice of cheap cigarettes.

The man who sat opposite to him, at the other end of the table, was unmistakably English. He was smoking a briar pipe, and though his clothes—neither new nor fashionably cut—were distinctly Parisian, his fair hair, blue eyes and rather heavy yellow moustache were eloquent of his nationality. He was bending over a large sheet of drawings on tracing paper with strained and careful attention.

He looked up suddenly, removed the pipe from his mouth, and began speaking in a torrent of French so perfect that he might very well have passed for a Parisian.

"Emile, I think I have it at last. The position of neutrality varies with the type of the machine owing to the fact of armature reaction, which distorts the magnetic field. We must therefore connect the commutating poles in series with the armature, when their windings will carry the full armature current."

Deschamps nodded, thought for a moment, and a quick technical discussion began between the two men, the sheet of drawings being pushed from one to the other, marked and annotated in the margin with pencil.

Suddenly Deschamps leant back in his chair.

"Yes," he said, "there can be no doubt about it. We're on the track, if we have not already discovered the most revolutionary theory in wireless telegraphy that the world has known as yet! What we know now, at nine o'clock on a November evening in a power station in Paris, might alter the whole course of life and society all over the world."

The Englishman nodded, with less excited but perfectly sincere agreement.

"Very well, then," cried Deschamps, "will the world ever benefit by our three years' work, our marvellous discovery? No! We're two poor devils, junior engineers of this company on two hundred and fifty francs a month. In all France no one will listen to us, and in all England also, as you have discovered. And why?"

"Oh, what is the use, Emile?" Gregory replied, cutting short his friend. "We have talked it over too many times. It's no good making a song about it. We have not got the money to carry out our experiments thoroughly and to construct our models, twenty thousand pounds—five hundred thousand francs, my friend! And as we shall never get that, no one will listen to us and it will remain for someone else to make our discovery when we're—either when we're dead or still nursing Thierry dynamos at a few francs a day."

As he spoke he rolled up the sheet of drawings and, with a deep sigh, thrust it into the inner pocket of his coat.

"Come along," he said; "we had better be getting home. It is more comfortable there than here, at any rate; and there's still one bottle of Maçon."

They left the little alcoved room, walked slowly down the hall, with a word or two to the foreman, and passed out into the office, where the engineer who was to succeed them and watch through the night was smoking with the timekeeper.

Then, arm in arm, they passed into Paris.

They were a strange couple, these two. Basil Gregory was the son of a Cambridge tutor, who early in his career had gone to Paris as the English master of a famous Lycée. He had married a Frenchwoman, who had died five years after Basil's birth. The boy had been brought up in Paris until he was old enough to go to one of the lesser public schools of England, which was all his father could afford for him. He won a science scholarship from his school to Cambridge, had worked hard and played hard at the University, until an unfortunate encounter with a proctor during one of the evenings of the "May Week" had caused him to be sent down for ever and a day. It was a stupid affair enough, but the hot-headed young man's treatment of the guardian of University morals had been too flagrant to be passed over.

Basil had returned to Paris, spent six months as a pupil in the school for electrical engineers, and had finally been apprenticed to the Société Générale. At the end of his apprenticeship his father had died, leaving him his blessing and a couple of hundred pounds. From that time to this, and he was now exactly the same age as his friend Deschamps, the young man had worked as a junior engineer at the central power station. His salary was ten pounds a month. There were innumerable people before him, and his prospects seemed absolutely nil.

As for Deschamps, he was the son of a bankrupt wine merchant of Marseilles. With a remarkable taste for science and an especial interest in electricity, he had come to Paris—after an apprenticeship at the electrical station of Monte Carlo—and was in precisely the same state as Basil Gregory. The two young men had become friends at once. Each recognised in the other a brain above the average. Both of them were intensely interested in their work, both of them had the temper of mind which flouts accepted theories and ever presses forward to new and epoch-making discovery. They were pioneers, and knew it. Without conceit, without any self-deception, they were quietly certain of their own powers. They had worked together, spending every moment of their spare time and every franc they could afford upon a new and original development in wireless telegraphy. They had arrived at a point when they were both convinced that they had wrested an entirely new secret from Nature, and at this point they found, as so many inventors and pioneers have found in the past, that the way was absolutely barred for want of capital. In their hands they were sure they held the talisman of fortune and undying renown. It was useless to them for want of money.

This night in Paris was bitter cold. Moreover, an infrequent and dreaded occurrence in Paris, a dense fog lay over the city. These Parisian fogs are not the sulphurous, pea-soup discomforts of London, but they are almost as unpleasant, and quite as upsetting to ordinary life and comfort. A dank, grey mist, opaque and wet, seems to rise from the Seine, spread outwards in evergrowing density and chill, until all the central quarter of Paris is hidden and throttled by it.

"Diable!" Deschamps said, coughing, as they left the power station behind them. *"Une vraie brume Anglaise."*

Gregory shrugged his shoulders. "It is pretty bad," he said, "and we can't see a yard in front of our noses. Still, if you had experienced a London 'particular,' Emile—well, then you *would* know!"

There was a silence between the young men as they tramped away to the Latin Quarter, where they shared a room in a little fifth-rate hotel not far from the Quai Voltaire. The night was bitterly cold, certainly not inviting conversation, and the thoughts of the pair were cold and bitter in harmony with the night. Genius is rarely unconscious of its power. Basil Gregory and Emile Deschamps were not in the least conceited, but each knew in his heart of hearts that already they approached those heights upon which Tesla and Edison dwelt. They saw the top of the mountain bathed in glorious sunshine, but between them and it there was a great gulf only to be bridged by money.

Basil Gregory's case was, perhaps, the worse of the two, for Basil was in love. Ethel McMahon, the pretty Irish girl, who was English mistress in a young ladies' school in the Fauberg St. Honoré, held all his heart, but she, like him, was poor and friendless, and out of her wretched salary supported an invalid mother, who was a martyr to one of the cruellest forms of arthritis.

The young man ground his teeth in fury against Fate, as he strode by his companion's side. Suddenly he began to talk rapidly, and with a true Parisian vehemence.

"I shouldn't mind so much, Emile, if we wanted money for the reason that such a lot of fellows of our age want it. But we don't. We don't want to play the giddy goat"—*faire la bête* was the French he used—"we don't want to enjoy ourselves in the usual silly way. We only want the world to recognise us for what we are. We want to benefit the whole world, Emile, and for ourselves all we ask is recognition and sufficient to live in comfort."

"It's true," Deschamps replied. "For myself, a flat in central Paris, a motor car to take me quickly to my experimental works, money to travel to America to see all the developments of electricity there—that is all I ask."

"It's much the same with me," the other returned, "except that I want to get married as well and give poor dear Ethel a happy life, and her mother the comforts that she needs. And yet—oh, I'd give anything, *anything*, to get the money for our experiments."

Deschamps shrugged his shoulders. "Well, we cannot rob a church," he said, "and the penalties for any sort of burglary are most unpleasant in France. We must even wait upon Fortune. After all, *mon ami*, our chance may yet come. Every day we read in the newspapers of strange strokes of fortune coming to people. I cannot believe that we shall never have our opportunity. Who knows!"—he threw out an arm with one of the theatrical gestures habitual to men of the South—"who knows but that this very night some very great thing will happen to us! Faith! faith! We must believe, and Fortune will be kind to us. She ever turns away coldly from a faint and despairing heart!"

He took his fancy and embroidered it in a stream of words so vivid, hopeful and full of fancy that he half persuaded the more phlegmatic Englishman by his side. Basil listened in silence, warmed a little, and was not quite so hopeless as he had been. Then, out of mere shame at his own feeling, he stemmed the other's torrent of words.

"That is all very well," he said grimly, "but meanwhile Dame Fortune seems to have deserted us worse than ever. While we have been talking nonsense we have missed our way, and if you can tell me where we are, or whereabouts the Hotel Buonaparte may be lying, I shall be extremely obliged to you, Monsieur Deschamps of the rosy hopes!"

The two men stopped. It was as Gregory had said. That they were near the Seine was obvious, because of the intenser thickness of the fog, but there was no doubt that they had entirely lost their direction. The white mist was as thick as wool, wet, motionless, and icy. Where they stood, upon the pavement, and half-way down a mean, narrow street, the blurred contours of which were perfectly unfamiliar, hardly a sound could be heard. Wheel traffic there was none. The hum of fog-gripped Paris came to them as if from an incredible distance; there was not even a footstep to be heard.

Once more Deschamps shrugged his shoulders. "*Bien*," he said; "yes, we have certainly 'done it this time,' as you say. I have no notion where we are. I am as cold as an iceberg and as hungry as a goat."

They stood looking at each other, though the face of each was an indistinct, pale glimmer. They had gone a little too much to the west, and had lost themselves in the narrow network of mean streets somewhere behind the École Militaire. To reach the Latin Quarter would need considerable ingenuity upon a clear evening when the lamps shone brightly. At the moment it seemed a sheer impossibility.

"Shall we turn back?" Deschamps asked.

Gregory shook his head. "No," he replied. "You pretend to be so intimate with the habits of Fortune, and yet you ask a question like that! Let us go on. We are bound to find our way somehow into some street where there is more life and movement. And if we meet a gang of Apaches—well, we are neither of us weaklings, and we have got a couple of good walking-sticks. Forward, Emile Deschamps! We go to seek our fortune!" And as he said it he laughed with bitter cynicism.

They went on, but as they did so, and when they had walked a hundred and fifty yards or more, the street in which they were grew even narrower and more silent. Every now and then, at long distances, there was a gas lamp, but its yellow light was so muffled by the fog that it hardly penetrated for more than a yard or so, and if the prismatic colours the light made upon the mist were beautiful, they were quite useless to two young gentlemen hungry for supper and far from home.

Emile Deschamps took a box of matches from his pocket, wax ones, which burned immediately without the spectral blue flame of the more general Government article. He lit one—there was not a breath of wind—and held it above his head. The two men walked onwards for a few yards while the feeble light lasted, carefully scrutinising the tall houses which abutted on the pavement. They seemed to consist of small workshops and factories, now blind and deserted. Another match brought them to a stretch of wide wood paling, beyond which rose dim objects seeming like giant mounds or pyramids, and even as the match flickered out it threw its light upon a painted sign.

"Ah!" Deschamps said suddenly. "Now I know! We are in the wood quarter! This is a street of *chantiers de bois*."

Basil groaned. "Good heavens!" he said, "then we *have* come out of our way," for he knew instantly that they had penetrated to that part of Paris where the huge wood-sheds were, where the firewood is cut and stored, and timber for all other purposes is kept. All around them were the great wood stacks and deserted yards. There was not a sound to be heard, and doubtless the few watchmen that were on guard were comfortably sleeping over the stoves in their huts.

"Go on, or turn back?" Deschamps said.

Gregory took a franc from his pocket, and spun it under a gas lamp to which they had just come up. "Heads we go on," he said, and as the coin fell upon the back of his hand, sure enough the figure of Liberty was uppermost.

"That settles it," he said, and once again the boots of the friends rang upon the pavement.

They had travelled for some fifty yards or so, when a rather brighter light than usual came into their view.

"By Jove!" Gregory said, "an electric light at last! I know current is supplied to this neighbourhood because there have recently been representations in the Chamber of Deputies as to the necessity for supplying current to all this part owing to the inflammable nature of the wood. The Société is interested in the matter. I saw some correspondence about it in the office, but the people in this part are very conservative and none too well off, either. Let us have a look."

They came up to the light. It was not a street lamp, but projected from above the door of an old and rather shabby building, and immediately beneath it was a trade sign which could easily be read in the stronger illumination. This was the sign:

CARNET FRÈRES,

GRAVEURS SUR BOIS BOISAGE.

"Well, here's something," Gregory said, "and by the fact that the light is still on, one may suppose that there is someone inside. It is a wood-engraver's and wood-turner's workshop, you see. Yes, the door's actually open! We will go in and inquire where we are."

As he spoke he pushed open a swing door of wood, from which the paint was peeling, and, followed by Deschamps, entered without further ado.

CHAPTER II

The two young men were conscious of a pleasant sensation of warmth as the door swung to behind them.

They found themselves in a narrow passage, and immediately to their left was a glass window like the window of a conciergerie, one panel of which was open and looked into a dingy office lit by a single gas jet. There was nothing in the office but a safe, a desk round the wall, and some high stools, while a cheap French clock ticked from a bracket upon the wall.

"At any rate, whoever they are, they have not gone," said Deschamps with satisfaction. "Now we shall be all right," and as he said it he rapped loudly with his knuckles upon the little counter in front of the glass partition. They waited for nearly half a minute, but there was no response. Finally Gregory took his walking stick and beat a tattoo upon the counter. The sound of his knocking had hardly died away when footsteps were heard in the distance. They grew nearer, and a door leading into the office behind the partition was pushed open, and a strange and rather startling figure entered.

This was a little man not more than four feet high, wearing a round black cap of alpaca, a green baize apron, and a huge circular pair of spectacles. His face was brown and shrivelled. A fine network of wrinkles was all over it, and beneath the alpaca cap were straggling locks of dingy white. The nose which supported the pair of grotesque horn spectacles was large and bird-like, the mouth below was innocent and kindly.

The little man, in short, looked exactly like the traditional toy or clock maker of Nuremberg in a comic opera, stepping clean off the stage to greet the new-comers.

He looked up at them with a courteous but inquiring glance as he turned up the gas jet and they saw him more clearly. Then, placing two soiled and wrinkled, but delicate and capable, hands upon the counter, he made an odd bow.

"Messieurs?" he said, in a thin, piping voice.

Deschamps raised his hat. "I am sorry to say that my friend and I have lost our way," he began. "The fog is very thick to-night, and it is growing thicker and thicker. We have come quite out of our route, and do not know where we are. We are trying to get to the Latin Quarter, where we live."

The little man raised his hands, and as he did so, both young men noticed how prehensile and delicate they were—the hands of a master workman.

"*Mon Dieu!*" he said, "but you are very far out of your way, indeed, gentlemen. This is the Rue Petite Louise. It is not a thoroughfare at all. It is only a cul-de-sac, which winds among the wood-yards. Between here and the Latin Quarter the district is very congested, and you might walk about all night in a fog like this unless you could find a taxi-cab."

"I am afraid there won't be any cabs abroad to-night in this part of Paris," Gregory broke in. "Well, we must just take our chance. I thank you very much, monsieur."

"But it is impossible!" the odd little creature said with a tiny shriek. "The hour is already late, gentlemen; the fog, as you say, grows thicker every moment. And, look you, on a night like this there will be all sorts of robbers abroad. It is most unsafe."

Deschamps shrugged his shoulders. "Doubtless," he said, "but there is nothing else for it."

The little man on the other side of the counter peered at them anxiously through his great round spectacles. "But, yes," he said, in a plaintive bleat, "if affairs call you home, monsieur—doubtless madame will be distressed—then, indeed you must go, but— —"

Deschamps laughed. "No, we have no business; we have finished our work for the day, and we are not married; still— —"

"The matter is settled," said the old gentleman, with a child-like smile. "You will do me the honour of coming into our workshop immediately. We have a fire there, soup, bread, and *vin ordinaire* are ready, and there is enough for all. My brother will be as pleased as I am to have the honour of offering you hospitality on such a night. No"—he waved his hands in reply to a murmur of protest from Deschamps—"we could not let you go. Stay with us until the morning, and we will do our best to make you comfortable as may be."

Eager, chirping and twittering like an excited bird, the odd, old fellow unlatched a half-door, pushed up the counter-flap and bowed them into the little office. In a moment they had passed through it into a long, narrow room with a high roof which seemed to be of glass.

The place was lit by a huge fire of coal and wood, which glowed in an open hearth, and by the side of it was a small forge. The red light streamed out in a mysterious radiance upon a workshop crowded with tools, long tables, stacks of rare and polished woods, and here and there an unfamiliar machine.

The only other light came from two candles stuck upon a bench in their own grease, and the whole effect was startlingly curious and unexpected. It was as picturesque as some carefully set scene upon the stage, and seemed utterly removed from the modern life of a great city. The red light of the fire left distant corners of the workshop in black, impenetrable shadow, making it seem of vast extent.

Around the fire, however, the half-circle of light it threw out showed everything with great distinctness.

Gregory and Deschamps looked round them with bewildered eyes, and then, simultaneously, they gasped.

Rising from an old oak chair, emerging from its depths rather, there came another little man towards them.

In every particular he was exactly like their guide. In that bizarre light, at any rate, hardly anyone could have told them apart, and as he stepped forward he peered at them through identical round spectacles.

"My brother, Edouard," said the old man who had welcomed them. "Edouard, these gentlemen have lost their way in the fog. They are very far from their home, and it would be dangerous for them to seek it to-night without a proper guide. I have accordingly asked them to come in, and begged of them to share our simple supper, and to wait till the fog goes."

"But I am enchanted!" said the second little man, settling his round alpaca cap upon his head and waving his right arm in an expressive pantomime of welcome. "But this is most fortunate, gentlemen. Supper is nearly ready; come to the fire. Charles and myself are delighted to be of service."

The sudden transition from bitter cold and the grey blanket of the fog to this extraordinary place bewildered both the engineers. It was almost as if they moved among the scenes of some fantastic dream, as they sat down upon a bench by the fire, removed their damp hats and overcoats, and looked around them.

Was this really modern Paris? Who were these two kindly, dwarf-like creatures who had welcomed them into this warm, secret place, which seemed like a cavern of the gnomes?

Suddenly Basil Gregory became conscious that "my brother Charles" was standing before him and speaking.

"We are the Carnet Frères," he was saying, "and twin brethren also! I noticed, monsieur, you were startled as Edouard came to greet you. And, *naturellement*, this old workshop of ours is something out of the ordinary way. But we have lived and worked here for twenty years, my brother and I—we have a sleeping-room at the back—and what we do for our living is a small and specialised branch of the wood-worker's trade, and we have the monopoly of it."

Basil bowed. "My comrade, Monsieur Emile Deschamps," he said. "I, myself am an Englishman, and my name is Gregory."

The hands of Brother Charles flickered in front of him. "But it is wonderful!" he said with the pleased surprise of a child with a new toy. "You are English to look at, monsieur. There is nothing of the Latin about you; and yet you speak French as well as I do."

"I have lived nearly all my life in Paris," Basil answered with a smile.

"That accounts for it," the other twittered. "And now I see Brother Edouard is preparing the meal. *Mon Dieu,* Edouard, how hungry these poor gentlemen must be!"

An iron pot was hooked over the fire—a steaming pot, a pot of fragrant promise. From it into stout china bowls Brother Edouard was ladleing thick brown soup.

Brother Charles wheeled round to the long work-bench and began to cut thick slices of bread, to rattle spoons, parade a somewhat dingy cruet, set flat-footed glasses by each bowl, and uncork two bottles of *vin ordinaire*.

Overflowing with hospitality and the most charming child-like excitement, the odd, bird-like hosts served the soup and poured out that cheap table-wine of Paris, which is exactly the colour of permanganate of potash and water.

Basil and Emile sat down without further ado, and for five minutes there was a happy silence. The *pot-au-feu* was rich and nourishing. The wine was exactly that to which the friends themselves were accustomed. The fog and the cold in the ridiculous, inhospitable outside world was quite forgotten, and it seemed as if some malignant fog-curtain in their own brains had now rolled up and disappeared.

The faces of the two young men lost their pinched and discontented look. Anxiety faded from their eyes, and as they passed their cigarette cases to their hosts, and four thin blue spirals of smoke rose out of the red light to be lost in the shadows of the roof, Basil Gregory and Emile Deschamps had lost all thought of care.

It seemed quite natural, perfectly in the order of things, to be sitting there with their fantastic and courteous entertainers in a strange, mediæval setting—two starving wayfarers upon a hillside, taken in to the cave of the kindly gnomes, or the workshop of beneficent magicians.

"Your cigarettes are of the best tobacco, monsieur," said Charles Carnet. "*Au bon fumeur!* My brother and I had expected to spend a lonely evening. Here's to the fortunate chance that brought us guests!"

He tossed off a thimbleful of the purple wine with a flourish.

"But I could wish, gentlemen," said his brother, "that we could have entertained you better, I am afraid we are old-fashioned in our ways, and prefer a simple menage. At any rate, there might have been more light upon the scene. The fire is all very well, but these two candles give hardly any illumination. As a rule, our workshop is lit with electric light, and we also use the current for our lathe. An hour ago, however, there was a 'fizz' and a 'spit' from that porcelain box there in the casing of the electric wires, and, behold! the light went and the lathe will not work. It has happened before, and we must now wait till to-morrow for the electrician to come from the works and put it right for us."

Basil Gregory laughed. "Fate hath many surprises, Monsieur Carnet," he said, "and surely we have been specially sent to your assistance to-night! My friend and I are both electrical engineers attached to the superintending station of the Société Générale at Mont Parnasse. I expect I know what has happened. And I shall be very much mistaken if I cannot put it right for you in two or three minutes."

The little gentlemen were on their feet in a second, chirping and twittering with pleasure.

"*Tiens!* Edouard," said Brother Charles, "we have been entertaining angels unawares!"

"You are right, Charles," said Brother Edouard. "Angels of light."

Gregory and Deschamps went to the opposite wall of the workshop, moving cautiously among the benches, litter of wood-blocks and tools. Deschamps held one of the candles while Gregory deftly unscrewed the round porcelain cap of the cut-out. It was as he suspected, and he pulled out the semi-circular china bridge from its brass clips and showed it to his hosts.

"It is quite simple," he said. "Between this brass screw and this, there is always a soft wire made of tin and lead—fusible metal, we call it. All the current which lights your lamps and runs your lathes passes through the insulated copper wires, but it has to pass through the little lead wire as well. From some reason or other the current gets too strong and might heat the wires and create a fire; the little lead wire strung on this half-circle melts with the heat, and the current is shut off. That was the spitting noise you heard."

He plunged his hand into a side pocket and withdrew a small coil of fuse wire, which every practical engineer carries, and a screwdriver. In half a minute he had fixed three inches of the soft lead wire into the bridge, and snapped the bridge into its place in the box.

There was a click as the blocks came home, and then, in an instant, the long workshop was flooded with white light, while at the far end of it the motor, and the lathe it drove, began to hum and clatter with a sudden, disconcerting noise.

Edouard Carnet ran to the lathe and pulled down the tumbler switch. The noise stopped, but the brilliant illumination remained, and entirely changed the aspect of the room.

The great fire glowed a dull red now. The shadows shrivelled up into the corners and disappeared. Every object in the workshop was distinct and well-defined.

"A thousand thanks, monsieur," said the little men. "Another glass of wine! We will go back to the fireside and drink in light and comfort."

The four of them found their way back to their seats, and began to talk again. The eyes of the newcomers, however, were straying round the workshop with a curiosity they could hardly disguise. The place had been mysterious before, and strangely picturesque in the half light. It was mysterious no longer, but a picturesqueness lingered still, while there was much that neither of them were able to understand.

Suddenly Deschamps gave an exclamation. His eye had fallen upon something which interested and excited him, something which called up golden visions.

"*Tiens!*" he cried, jumping up from his seat, and going over to the adjacent table. "And what have we here?"

Upon the table was a circular basin—rather larger than an ordinary washing basin—beautifully made of polished black ebony, and with a rim that curved over upon the inside. Upon the inward curve of the basin, at regular distances, were diamond-shaped bosses of bright metal, while the whole of the bottom of the instrument consisted of a series of tin compartments painted black and red alternately, each compartment having a number painted upon it in white. These compartments were fixed to a moving disc, which could be rapidly rotated by means of a silver upright terminating in a sort of capstan, and rising above the sides of the bowl in the exact centre.

Emile Deschamps knew very well what this was. He was of the South. He had been born near that fairy city on the Mediterranean where the Goddess of Chance rules supreme.

"Then you make roulette wheels?" he cried, turning excitedly to the two little men. "But this one is superb! It is larger than you can buy in the shops. It is full size indeed—exactly as they are used at Monte Carlo!"

With fingers that actually trembled, the young man twirled the silver capstan, and immediately the painted slots in the bowl became merged in a trembling blur of colour, as the disc revolved noiselessly, but at great speed.

"It is perfect!" Emile went on, with a chuckle of excitement and delight. "It runs as sweetly and truly as those in the Casino itself! Basil, look here! See how delicate and beautiful this work is!"

The brothers Carnet had risen to their feet also, and were standing side by side. Their bird-like faces were wreathed with gratified smiles. They bowed together like a grotesque toy.

"Messieurs," said Brother Edouard, "we thank you for what you have said. The wheel is, indeed, as you say, a masterpiece! But it would be odd if it were not so, for, for twenty years my brother and myself have done nothing else than make just these wheels. Every single piece of it is our handiwork. We forge the nickel for the pivot and capstan, and we silver-plate it ourselves. We select the wood, we turn it—no other hands but ours touch the wheels. Brother Charles here even turns the ivory balls." He stepped up to the table, pulled out a long drawer, and lifted from it a walnut box lined with green baize, in which were a dozen small balls of ivory, the size of a large marble.

"See!" he cried; "these also!"

Basil had been examining the delicate and beautifully made machine with great interest while the Carnets had been speaking. He also had an eye for perfect workmanship, and it needed not the excited enthusiasm of his friend for him to realise that he saw it here.

At the same time, he could not quite understand the sort of fever into which the sight of the roulette wheel had thrown Deschamps. It seemed exaggerated to the Englishman. Here was good workmanship, it was true. But why this torrent of excited words?

"For twenty years!" Deschamps cried. "Then; indeed, monsieur, that explains it! But surely it cannot pay you to devote your life to this work, though it is certainly the finest I have ever seen, and far superior to anything one can buy in the shops!"

The two brothers chuckled; and then Charles took up the tale.

"Our wheels are not for sale," he said. "I must let you into a little secret, which, as our guests and men of honour, you will preserve. My brother and I make all the roulette wheels for the Casino at Monte Carlo. We have been employed by the Administration for many, many years. As you may well conceive, it is important that these machines should be perfect in every detail. Millions of francs depend upon it. We are retained at a large figure to construct the wheels. Every two years all the wheels at Monte Carlo are changed. There are twelve roulette tables generally in use. Every two years we send twelve wheels and the old ones are returned to us to be broken up. We can just make twelve within the two years. This one is the last of the new batch which will be dispatched to the south in three days in charge of two commissionaires from Monaco, who will never leave them out of their sight until they arrive at their destination."

Basil listened to this explanation with interest. He had never been to Monte Carlo, though, in common with the rest of the world, he had heard many fabulous tales of the great gambling centre of the world. He saw, however, that Emile's imagination was profoundly stirred, and he listened, half dreamily, to the quick fire of eager questions and courteous answers which passed between Deschamps and his hosts.

When this had a little died down, Emile turned to him and noticed his half-abstracted, half-amused expression.

"Ah, *mon ami,*" he said, "you wonder at me! This leaves you cold. It means nothing to you. To me, who have been, I myself, in those glittering halls of Chance, upon the edge of the Mediterranean, this machine brings intoxicating visions. It tells of men and women at the last gasp of hope, ruined in fortune, friendless, and with the whole face of the world set against them like a wall of polished brass. It tells me of a man like this entering through the great doors and issuing forth again within a few short hours, rich beyond his rosiest dreams, able to command all that life has to offer, the divine sense of power flowing in his veins, the cold brass wall gone and in its place a garden of roses! See!"

With a swift motion of his hands he picked up one of the little ivory balls and twirled the capstan in the disc. The painted slots began to revolve, more slowly than before.

Then, and obviously with a practised hand, Emile Deschamps held the ball between the thumb and two first fingers of his right hand, gave a swift motion of his wrist, and the little ivory cylinder whirled round the top of the basin under the overhanging lip, with that curious droning sound that no one who has ever heard it can quite forget.

Click! crack! crack! The speed of the ball lessening, it was now rattling upon the diamond-shaped bosses on the side of the bowl, losing momentum with every moment, until it dropped upon the revolving disc below—revolving in the opposite direction to itself.

And now there was a succession of sharp taps, as the little ball was tossed by the edges of the slots hither and thither, furiously jumping from one to the other, flung back for an instant upon the sloping side of the basin, returning to its mad career over the slots.

And then—a sudden final click as it fell to rest. Silence!

Immediately Deschamps put his finger upon the top of the capstan and stopped the revolutions of the slots.

"Seven—red!" he cried. "Ah! if I had put but nine little golden louis upon that number, within a quarter of a minute I should have been richer by six thousand three hundred francs, more than twice what I earn in a whole year, Basil! In twenty little seconds! Now, do you see what this thing may mean?"

Basil found himself strangely affected by his friend's enthusiasm. He knew nothing of roulette. He had occasionally seen a small wheel in a toy shop, but this so concrete illustration of the game startled him more than he would have been willing to admit.

The thin voice of Edouard Garnet broke in. "Yes, monsieur," he said, "that is one vision, but there are others. Who should tell of those unhappy men who have followed the Goddess of Chance even to the very gates of death, until they have opened and closed upon them at last. Somewhere in the kingdom of Monaco there is a hidden graveyard; none know where it is. And in that dishonoured plot lies hundreds of nameless ones, who have yielded up their all—happiness, honour, life—to the ebony basin."

Basil started. The words seemed to come strangely from the actual artificer of the wheel of fortune. Deschamps also looked curiously at the little man, whose face had suddenly gone grey and whose voice trembled. "But, monsieur," he said, in a hesitating voice.

The other made a gesture with his hand. "Yes, yes," he replied, "I well know what you would say—such words come strangely from me or from my brother. But, monsieur"—he tapped the rim of the bowl with a thin hand—"this is the very last of these engines of hell that I or Charles will ever make!"

He paused, struggling with some deep emotion. "We had a nephew," he continued, "my brother and I; the only relative left to us in the world. We loved him as if he had been a son. We saved, invested, and worked solely for him. We are rich, monsieur! Not only have our earnings been large, but we have saved, and invested our savings in safe rents. All, all was to have been his. Aristide was young, clever, and, backed by the fortune we could leave him, would have taken a high place in the world. He had gone to Marseilles on business for us, entrusted with a considerable sum of money. Some friends took him to Monte Carlo—it was only three months ago. He lost this money of ours at the tables—lost it by means of one of the very wheels we had made—and in despair he killed himself, though God knows how gladly we would have forgiven him. We have now completed our last contract for the Administration. We have resigned our position, and for the future others shall make the wheels. We will touch them no more."

"Never again," Charles Carnet echoed his brother, but he looked lovingly at the glittering thing upon the table nevertheless. "No one will make the wheels like us again," he said with a sigh.

The four men, oddly assorted as they were, gathered round the fire once more. There was but little conversation now. They gazed into the glowing heart of coals and wood-blocks, each busily occupied with his own troubled thoughts.

Basil Gregory, warmed and comfortable as he was in body, felt very low in spirits. One of those moments had come to him when life seems a spoilt and futile thing. The future stretched before him in imagination like some great Essex marshland at evening, when the colour fades out of everything, the leaden tides creep inwards from the sea, and the curlews pipe to each other with melancholy voices, like souls sick for love. There was nothing, nothing! A dreary round of ill-paid mechanical duties, a long engagement which would probably never end in marriage, one of the most epoch-making inventions the world could ever know, locked up in his mind and that of his friend, Emile Deschamps.

Thus the thoughts of the poor Englishman, Basil Gregory, as he gazed into the rose-pink and amethyst heart of the fire.

The two old men were sadly remembering the recent loss of the bright-faced boy that had meant everything in their narrow, patient lives.

Sadness lay like a veil upon the faces of all three.

But Emile Deschamps' face was not sad. It was set and rigid. Not a feature of it moved. The brow was wrinkled and knotted with thoughts. There was a fixed and smouldering fire in the eyes. Once Basil looked at his friend and wondered what intense and concentrated thought was burning and glowing in the great executive brain of the Southerner. Had he known, had an inkling of it reached him, he would have leapt to his feet in the wildest excitement he had ever known.

For, indeed, the fickle Goddess of Chance was abroad this night, and had led their footsteps to this secluded workshop. Unseen, unfelt by any save only Emile Deschamps, she was hovering in the room where the wheels of her votaries were made.

About dawn a low wind arose and wailed around the quarter of the wood-turners. The deep mist vanished as grey light began to filter in through the glass roof of the workshop. With many thanks the two young men bade their hosts farewell, and went out into the chill morning air.

A pressing invitation to come again whenever they liked, piped in unison by Brother Charles and Brother Edouard, was the last sound they heard as their feet echoed up the deserted street towards the great main thoroughfares of Paris.

CHAPTER III

The next day was cold, but bright and sunny. From ten o'clock in the morning until *déjeuner* at twelve o'clock, Ethel McMahon endeavoured to instil some rudimentary knowledge of English into the minds of the fifteen-year-old daughters of prosperous tradesmen of the Luxembourg district at the academy for young ladies of the Demoiselles de Custine-Seraphin, two elderly ladies in whom parsimony and the proprieties struggled for mastery.

With many a sigh and shrug of disgust her demure charges had struggled with the intricacies of our language, had conjugated the verb "to love" in unexpected fashions, had laboriously assimilated the information that "ze weadder is going to be ver' fin to-day," and so forth.

At twelve, together with her fellow-teachers, Mademoiselle Marie and Mademoiselle Augustine de Custine-Seraphin, Ethel had taken the second breakfast of thin soup, pallid mutton, and stale *tartines au confiture*. At one she was free—free till nine o'clock in the evening. And as she came downstairs from her room dressed to go out, her face was so radiant and changed in expression that Mademoiselle Marie de Custine-Seraphin tossed her head as the girl passed, and gave it as her undoubted opinion to her sister that *la jeune anglaise* was certainly going to do more than spend a quiet afternoon and evening with her invalid mother.

"Figure to yourself, Augustine; her face was of the most beaming, her eye had sparkle, her cheeks were colour of rose. *Ca fait un amant, n'est-ce pas?*"

"A la jeunesse, comme à la jeunesse," her sister replied with a shrug, and went on making up the account of Mademoiselle Hortense Dubois, the well-to-do butcher's daughter who was leaving school that quarter.

Ethel McMahon hurried out of the quiet street in which the school was situated, walking towards the Luxembourg.

She was a typically Irish girl in feature, with those dark-blue eyes, like hot Venetian water, that hair black as a bog-oak root, that complexion of cream and roses that is hardly seen anywhere outside the Isle of Unrest. She was tall and walked with a swing, as she threaded her way among the *chic* and mincing Parisiennes towards her mother's tiny flat in the Rue Paczensky.

Dull as the girl's life was, hard as she worked all day, her youth and vitality were stronger than the power of circumstances. Vivid and impulsive in all she did, a constant spring of hope welled up within her, and she was certain that sooner or later—she believed very soon—everything in her life would come right. Dear Basil would get some lucrative appointment, the great invention would be financed by some kindly millionaire who would appear in the nick of time. They would get married, her mother would be able to live in the far healthier air of the Alps, as the doctor had ordered. Day in and day out Ethel was convinced that all would be well, and whenever she saw her lover she comforted and inspirited him as if they were indeed husband and wife.

Mrs. McMahon's flat of two rooms and a kitchen was high up in the great drab block of buildings, and, small as it was, the rent, as is the case with all flats in Paris, was proportionately high.

As she entered the hallway Ethel was handed a bundle of letters by the concierge. She did not examine them at the moment, but ran lightly up the stairs to the flat.

Mrs. McMahon was seated by the window of the sitting-room. A lace pillow with its pins and reels of thread was upon the table before her, and her thin hands were moving quickly and deftly over it hither and thither.

It was Mrs. McMahon's specialty to copy old Valenciennes lace, which she did for a firm in the Rue de Rivoli. The labour was intense, the process wearingly long, but the few hundred francs earned during the year by this means helped to pay the rent.

She was a tall, faded woman. The hair, which had once been as black as her daughter's, was now scanty and iron-grey. All the light had faded from the blue eyes, and she was painfully thin. She returned her daughter's caresses without much animation, and sat back in her old-fashioned chair with her hands lying idly in her lap, gazing at the girl in a lack-lustre way as she moved quickly about the room, taking off her hat and stole of cheap fur, giving a touch to the furniture here and there, and putting a little bunch of dark-red asters, which she had bought, into a vase upon the dining-table.

"Well, Ethel, I suppose you have no news? I hope those old cats"—Mrs. McMahon was accustomed to refer to the Demoiselles de Custine-Seraphin in this way—"I hope those old cats have been behaving themselves better. I cannot think why you stay with them. Surely a girl with your knowledge of French as well as English, and with your appearance, could get something better to do. The salary they pay you is disgraceful."

Ethel shook her head brightly; this was an old ground of debate between herself and the querulous invalid. "My dear mother," she said, "I really cannot afford to wait for anything better to turn up. If I could, possibly I might get something better to do, but that would mean coming home for perhaps three or four months, and you know we cannot possibly afford that. While I am at the school, of course, I cannot go looking after another post. So I must make the best of it, that's all."

Mrs. McMahon coughed fretfully. "How horrified your poor dear father would have been," she said, "at the life you are leading now! It is my one consolation that Providence has spared him that!"

Ethel said nothing in answer, though she had her doubts upon the subject. The late Captain McMahon had retired from the Irish Guards soon after getting his company and marrying pretty Miss Persse of county Galway. There were not wanting those who said that his retirement was more or less compulsory owing to rather too pronounced successes while holding the bank at baccarat or chemin de fer. Be that as it may, Ethel's memory of her childhood in various more or less shady Continental resorts was by no means a pleasant one. Captain McMahon had been one of those people whose whole philosophy is summed up in the expression, "Hang it, the luck *must* turn!" He had wooed fortune wherever a casino or gambling hell was to be found upon the Continent of Europe; he had wooed her in vain; the luck never did turn.

However, it was doubtless owing to this persistent optimism inculcated by her father that Ethel herself was enabled to bear up against the drab monotony of her life. She also felt instinctively that "the luck must turn." As for Mrs. McMahon herself, while she affected a consistent despair and the gloomiest outlook upon the future, she secretly nourished the most extravagant hopes, and was as much a gambler in temperament as her husband had been in action. Only the most limited opportunities of exercising her passion were given her, but of these she took advantage to the full.

"I cannot think," the elder lady went on, "what that lover of yours can be about. Oh, I have nothing to say against Basil," she said hurriedly, as she saw Ethel's colour begin to rise, and her mouth to harden into mutiny. "Basil is a good fellow enough, and, of course, I know he is very clever at his electricity, and so on. He and that young Frenchman, Monsieur Deschamps, have no doubt got a fortune in their heads, as you are always telling me. All that I can say is that it seems likely to stay there. With your blood Ethel, for both the Persses and the McMahons rode straight for anything they wanted, I wonder at your choosing a boy like Basil, who seems to have no initiative, no dash. Ah, well! I suppose there are no soldiers of fortune nowadays. But, still, with your name and your appearance, I think you might have done better for yourself."

Ethel knew it was useless to answer anything to this. She let her mother run on until she was tired, and then began to make tea, with a little spirit kettle.

As she was doing this, she noticed the little pile of letters that the concierge had handed to her. The top one had not come by post, and was unstamped. Ethel knew the writing very well. It was that of the clerk who sent out demands and receipts for the rent at the office.

"Ah!" she said; "here is the receipt for the quarter's rent." She had given her mother the money to pay it some time ago, and without thinking what she was doing, she opened the envelope.

Mrs. McMahon rose from her seat in considerable agitation. Her hands trembled a little, and a bright colour came into her wan face.

"Why, mother," Ethel said in alarm, "this is not a receipt at all! This is a letter from the office saying that the rent is much overdue, and pressing for immediate payment. I gave you the money!" The words died away from her lips as she saw the old lady, a picture of embarrassment, standing before her.

"My dear," said Mrs. McMahon, in a shaking voice, "you really must allow me to manage the household finances in my own way. I am older and more experienced in life than you. I have temporarily—er—well, *invested* the rent money in the hopes, in the almost certainty, that in a day or so I shall be repaid a hundred-fold."

Ethel sat down at the table with a deep sigh. "Oh, mother!" she said in a pleading voice, "how could you, how could you really? I suppose that it is one of those wretched lotteries again. I should not like to think how many precious francs have been simply thrown away in the last year or two. Hundreds and hundreds. It is simply madness to spend two or three hundred francs on a ticket for one of the wretched things when we have hardly money for the necessaries of life."

The old lady began to cry weakly. "I did it for the best, Ethel," she said. "I am sure I thought that my bad luck could not go on much longer. I had such hopes this time."

Ethel saw her opportunity. While her mother was in this state of penitence she might perhaps make a lasting impression.

"Mother," she said, earnestly, "gambling nearly ruined my grandfather; it quite ruined father. We could not be much worse off than we are, but don't throw away the last thing that keeps us from absolute starvation. Do not destroy the roof over our heads! If there were only something in it, I should not so much mind. To win anything in these affairs robs nobody. But there never *is* anything in it, worse luck. From us, at any rate, the spirit of Chance has turned her head; gambling of any sort is ruin."

"It is—it is," the old lady sobbed, now thoroughly broken down. "Oh, that I had never been drawn into it, had never had the poison instilled into my blood! But this is the last time, Ethel, dear; it is the last time, I promise you. And how to pay the rent I do not know."

Ethel sighed heavily. The rent could be paid this time, she knew. She had been fortunate in securing some extra English lessons during the last quarter—lessons which were given privately to a girl of about her own age, and which had brought her in a few louis; but she had wanted this money so badly for clothes. It was dreadful to go out with Basil on their rather rare holidays and to look dowdy and shabby, as she was only too conscious of being. She knew—what pretty girl does not?—how important decent clothes are, and she longed that her lover should see her dressed like other maidens in the restaurants and minor places of amusement where he was able to take her. And now—that was another little dream gone. The old brown coat and skirt and the imitation astrachan muff and stole would have to do for the rest of the winter; there was bitterness in the thought which no man can fathom.

"Oh, well," she said in a dull voice, "I have saved up a little, and I suppose it will be enough for the rent. But, oh, mother, how could you do it!"

"Never again! never again!" wailed the old lady, and with a dull pain at her heart Ethel left the room and went into the little kitchen to fetch the tea things.

She was a little longer in the kitchen than she had anticipated. Tears were in her eyes also, and it required all her resolution and self-control to keep them back, and to preserve her ordinary composure. At last, with a heavy sigh and trying to twist her face into the semblance of a smile, she took up the tray and went back into the sitting-room, resolved to comfort her mother as well as she could.

Mrs. McMahon, to her daughter's immense surprise, was standing by the window, very erect, with all traces of recent tears and penitence absolutely gone from her face. There was a superior and almost haughty smile upon the old lady's lips.

Ethel stared in wild astonishment at this transformation.

"Put the things down, my dear," said Mrs. McMahon, in a calm and patronising voice. "Perhaps when you have heard what I have got to say, you will realise the wisdom of trusting to older and more experienced people. I do not blame you, Ethel; you are but a child after all and can know nothing of the world. But I do ask you to trust to the wisdom and judgment of your elders in future. If you do so, and allow yourself to be guided by me in everything, then we shall very soon be relieved from our present position, and be able to return to that place in society which our birth and connections warrant."

Ethel dropped the tray some inches upon the table with a crash. Her lower lip dropped. Her eyes were wide.

Mrs. McMahon looked down upon her daughter—she was slightly taller than Ethel when she stood erect—with a kindly and compassionate smile, as one looks at a beloved but tiresome and fretful child.

"I suppose," she said, "that a little sum of two thousand five hundred francs would be sufficient to pay the rent?"

Ethel gasped.

"I suppose," Mrs. McMahon continued, "that you would regard a return of a hundred pounds for an investment of ten fairly remunerative?"

Ethel murmured something or other, she hardly knew what.

Then Mrs. McMahon condescended to explain. Her eagerness burst through, her high comedy manner vanished.

"Oh, my dear, my dear!" she cried, "the luck has turned at last! After all these years! Look! look!"

With shaking hands she held out some papers to Ethel. A typewritten sheet was headed, "Königlich-Preussiche-Klassen-Lotterie," and stated in French that Mrs. McMahon, who had purchased the eighth of a ticket in the famous Berlin lottery, had thereby won a sum of 2,000 Marks German, or—was added in parentheses—2,500 francs. A pink draft upon the Crédit Lyonnais was enclosed for the sum.

"Oh, mother!" Ethel gasped, in the sudden shock, "two thousand five hundred francs! A hundred pounds!" And, quite forgetful of her former strictures, she hugged the trembling old lady again and again. "We are rich! we are rich!" she cried, and a vision crossed her mind of an inexpensive hat she had but lately seen in the Rue de Rivoli—a perfect duck of a hat!

They sat down to tea, and never was there a happier meal. Ethel was to meet Basil at six, and he was to take her out to dinner.

"Oh, mother," she said, "how delighted Basil will be to hear the news! I am so sorry I spoke as I did, but it all seemed so hopeless. I see now that I was wrong."

Mrs. McMahon smiled. "My dear," she said, "remember that it is a rule in life that nothing venture, nothing have. This money seems a great deal, no doubt, and it certainly more than repays all that I have spent to get it, so that we are on the right side, after all, as your poor dear father used to say. But it is a principle in these affairs—and you will admit now that I know something about them—always to follow up your luck. It is the people who do not do that who never deserve to have any, and very rarely do have any."

Ethel did not quite understand what the elder lady meant, but she nodded. "Go on, mother dear," she answered.

Mrs. McMahon, who for the last two or three minutes had been sitting lost in thought, turned to her daughter. Her face was grave, but it showed a strangely suppressed excitement, and there was an odd glimmer in her eyes. "First of all, dear," she said, "we must pay the rent. Your little savings will not be required, after all. You can renovate your wardrobe, and I will add something to help you. More especially, you will have to get a really good evening gown, and a smart hat to wear with it."

Ethel stared. "But, mother," she said, "surely that is an extravagance? I never go anywhere where a smart evening gown is wanted. And you know what such things cost."

"A smart evening gown," Mrs. McMahon went on, almost as if she were talking to herself. "We must spend as little as possible upon it, but it must be decent. For myself, I have something that will do—that is, in the first instance."

"What are you talking about, mother dear?" Ethel asked.

"Now listen, Ethel," her mother replied. "A chance has come to us. It may well be our one and only chance. We must grasp it, or let it go by for ever. Fortune always turns her face away from those who refuse to follow when she beckons. I have a plan. We must take Fortune at the flood, as I said. To begin with, we must tell Basil Gregory nothing whatever of this little bit of good fortune which has befallen us. You must not say a word to him about it, or even hint at it."

"Oh, but mother, he would be so delighted to know. I always share everything with Basil."

"No doubt," said Mrs. McMahon, "but in this case I want you to do nothing of the sort. You will know why in a moment. Basil, dear fellow as he is—I am sorry I made some petulant remarks about your engagement a few minutes ago—is an Englishman. Apart from his high scientific attainments, which have yet to be proved, by the way, Basil has all the Englishman's solidity and caution. He is not imaginative. He is not a man to risk anything upon a supreme chance. Now, regard the situation in which we are."

"We are free from all debt, at any rate," Ethel answered wonderingly; "and we shall have a nice little surplus in hand."

"You must look farther than that, my dear," said her mother, with the odd brightness in her eyes growing more marked than ever. "A hundred pounds is all very well. We may buy shares in other lottery tickets. We may even buy a whole ticket, but that is a single chance, and means a great deal of waiting. Since Fortune is smiling upon us there is another and surer way to court her favours. I have been thinking quickly, as I generally do when there is something important to be decided. With this money"—she began to speak slowly and impressively—"you and I can go to Monte Carlo. We can go by the slow train, third class. It will take us twenty-four hours, and not be very comfortable. But that I can endure, and if I can, then so can you. I know the Principality of Monaco very well. At Monte Carlo itself all the hotels and places are terribly expensive, and far beyond our means, but only a quarter of a mile away, in that part known as the Condamine, there are lots of quite inexpensive *pensions* which would serve our purpose very well."

"But what on earth are we to do in Monte Carlo? and how can I leave the school?"

"The school, my dear Ethel, is of minor importance. Nothing venture, nothing have. What we are to do at Monte Carlo is to turn what will remain of our hundred pounds into such a sum as will make us independent for the rest of our lives—a sum that will allow me to go to Switzerland, as the doctor ordered, that will start you comfortably in your married life with Basil Gregory."

The last shot told, and set the girl's pulses throbbing furiously.

"Oh, mother," she said, "if it were only possible!"

"It is perfectly possible, my dear Ethel," Mrs. McMahon returned, and there was such calm certainty in her tone that the eager girl, carried off her feet by the arrival of the lottery cheque, and the brilliant vista which was beginning to unveil itself, hardly questioned her mother's wisdom at all.

"I know Monte Carlo very well," said the old lady. "I was there often enough with your poor dear father. On one occasion he lost every penny he had at the tables there, and we were compelled to apply to the Administration for what they call the *viatique*—that is, a sufficient sum to pay our expenses back to Paris, from whence we had come. It is never refused. But, on looking back, I see how foolish both your father and I were. We played recklessly. We ignored the most elementary rules of chance. We were rightly punished. For many months now I have been dreaming of just such a chance as has come to us at last. I have been studying the new book written by a professor, who won large sums of money at Monte Carlo, in the interests of mathematics, on the Theory of Probabilities. I have gained much knowledge from it. I propose to utilise that knowledge very shortly."

"Then you have definite plans?" Ethel asked.

"Perfectly definite, my dear. I have only been waiting to put them into execution. The time has now arrived. We will get the necessary clothes—for in order to obtain the entrée to the Casino, one must be decently dressed—and we will go to Monte Carlo at once. Three days' careful play at roulette—for I do not intend to go near the *trente-et-quarante* tables—will either see us with a sufficient fortune for our needs or take all we have got. Even if it does, we shall be little worse off than we are at present. Nothing can take my hundred a year from me, and you will easily find another post. It may even be that you can obtain a week's leave of absence from those old cats. It is worth while trying, at any rate. If not, you must resign the whole thing. For my part, I feel fully confident that you will never have to go back to such dreary drudgery."

Confidence expressed in an authoritative tone by an elder is infectious. Confidence already backed up by an initial proof is more infectious still. Ethel McMahon's scruples, doubts and hesitations vanished utterly, and she threw herself wholeheartedly into her mother's scheme.

CHAPTER IV

At six o'clock Basil came for Ethel. Mrs. McMahon greeted him rather more kindly than usual, and he noticed it with some surprise, for he was always conscious that the old lady did not care much for him. A humble-minded man, and bitterly conscious of his unsuccessful life, he was certain that such a radiant being as Ethel was a thousand times too good for him, and was even inclined to acquiesce in the old lady's estimate in a way that provoked his fiancée enormously.

He noticed also that in addition to the access of kindliness, there was a distinct patronage in Mrs. McMahon's manner. Her usual despondency seemed to have disappeared. She spoke largely and vaguely of "the future." He could not understand it at all.

"What on earth has happened to your mother?" he asked Ethel, as they descended the stone stairs towards the street. "I never saw her so chirpy, darling."

Ethel hesitated for a moment. She was bright and animated herself, and she pressed his arm affectionately before replying. She was so accustomed to share her every hope and thought with her lover that she found it difficult to frame a suitable reply. "Oh, well, you know, mother has ups and downs like the rest of us," she said at length. "To-day she is in particularly good spirits."

Basil sighed. "I wish I had the recipe," he said; "try to get it from her. It would be particularly useful just now."

"Are you depressed, dear?" the girl asked.

"Horribly; things seem worse than ever. Oh, Ethel, darling, it is dreadful to say so, but I do not think we shall ever be married!"

"You are not to talk like that, Basil; it is perfectly ridiculous, and I won't have it. Look at me. Am I depressed?"

"No," the man answered, looking wonderingly at her. "You have caught your mother's mood. But the last time we were out together, if you remember, you were as sad as I. We walked about the Luxembourg Gardens for an hour bewailing our lot."

"Yes, and after dinner we were as happy as possible, and made all sorts of plans. We furnished the drawing-room that evening, I think—or was it the dining-room?"

Basil laughed, but there was no mirth in his laughter. "It doesn't matter much," he replied, "but to-night I do not think I could take any interest in the attics of our Castle in Spain. For that's what it is, dearest, at present, and that's what I am sure it will remain."

"I have told you before, Basil, that you are not to talk like that. I simply won't have it. *Entend-tu?* Has anything happened to make you feel more despondent than usual?"

"Well, not exactly, and yet in a way there has, though it is only a little thing."

"Tell me, dear."

"Oh, only that Deschamps has suddenly grown quite extraordinary in his manner. You know what absolute friends we were?"

"I know," she nodded. "Have I not been horribly jealous of you two at times, sitting correcting exercises in that dreadful school in the evening, and thinking of you two men talking away together without anyone to interrupt?"

Man-like, Basil Gregory did not quite appreciate the underlying feeling in this remark.

"It has simply kept me alive," he went on, "and kept hope burning within me to be with Emile Deschamps. You see, our invention is just as much his as mine. We have worked it out together as if with one mind. Our interests are absolutely identical."

"But I don't exactly understand what has happened, Basil."

"His manner has absolutely changed ever since last night, when we had quite an adventure, he and I."

"An adventure?" she asked quickly. "And what was that?"

In reply Basil told her the whole history of the fantastic night. He told it well, warming to the work as he did so, and she saw the picture unfold itself—the queer, bird-like little men, the huge workshop with its strange implements, the welcome hospitality.

"And then," he concluded, "it turned out that they were hereditary makers of the roulette wheels for the gambling at Monte Carlo. They have made them for ever so many years, and they were just employed upon the last wheel of all on that very night. They are going to resign their position. They have made sufficient money upon which to live, and a young nephew of theirs, who gambled at Monte Carlo with money that was not his own, and afterwards committed suicide, has disgusted them, very naturally, with the whole thing."

Ethel's reply amazed him.

They were approaching the Rue Crois de Petits Champs, and she stopped upon the pavement and positively clutched his arm.

"And will the wheel you saw actually be used at Monte Carlo?" she asked in a voice that had suddenly become almost breathless.

He nodded, too surprised to speak.

"And you touched it?"

"Oh, yes; I twirled the beastly thing round, if that's what you mean. But why all this interest?"

Again for a moment she answered nothing, though her face had grown suddenly pale from excitement.

"I cannot tell you," she said at length, "though it may seem strange to you. It is a sudden thought, that is all. And, oh, Basil, dear, I somehow believe that it is a good omen, that it means fortune for both of us. Oh, I'm certain of it."

"What a queer little darling you are!" he said, with a laugh at her earnest manner. "But we must not block up the pavement like this. Come along."

They went onwards to their destination, a quaint little restaurant known as the "Restaurant de l'Universe et Portugal," which they had discovered some weeks before, and where one could get a really excellent dinner for two francs fifty a head.

For the remaining three minutes of their walk neither of them said anything. Every pulse in Ethel's body was leaping with excitement.

The coincidence was too strange. She was not more superstitious than most people, though like most people she had an undefined though real belief in premonitions and omens. And in this case the wish was indeed father to the thought. She had been so carried away by the minor success of the ticket in the first instance, and by her mother's plan in the second, that Basil's story seemed almost a direct and miraculous confirmation of her hopes. When they were seated at their accustomed table in the corner of the quiet little restaurant, and a delicious *pot au feu* was before them, she began to ply her lover with eager questions, making him recount every detail of the previous evening. He told her all that she wished to know, but suddenly she noticed that his face was still sad, and his eyes dreamy and introspective.

She remembered with a pang of accusation what he had been saying about Emile Deschamps.

"Oh, Basil," she said with pretty penitence, "here am I bothering you about last night, and you have not even told me what you were going to about Monsieur Deschamps. You said something had depressed you—some change in him?"

"Well, it has," the young man replied. "When we got home in the early morning to our hotel we neither of us wanted to go to bed, so we lit the stove and sat up in my room. I could not get Emile to say a word. He absolutely refused to discuss the events in the Rue Petite Louise. He scowled at me when I tried to draw him into conversation, as if I were trying to do him some injury. I have never known him like that. After about an hour I lay down on the bed and went to sleep, till they brought our morning coffee.

"About ten we walked to the works together. We have been there all day till just before I came to fetch you. Upon the way Emile was just as moody and brusque as ever. As he did not want to talk about those two kindly little men, I thought I would try another tack, and I began to discuss a detail of our invention. It is an improvement upon what we have already done, and at ordinary times such a thing would never fail to interest him."

"And didn't he rise to that?" Ethel asked.

"Never a bit. And that disturbed me more than ever, for it is so unlike him. All day he has been the same. We usually go to *déjeuner* together at a little café close to the works. This morning he positively refused to come with me, and, when I asked why, he insulted me. He was like a bear with a sore head."

"And you went alone?"

"Yes, and I have been alone ever since, and have been brooding over the position and got myself into a thoroughly depressed state of mind."

"Well, never mind, dear," Ethel replied, "get out of it now. How good this omelette is! And the wine, too; really, I think the *vin ordinaire* here is better than anywhere else in Paris. Cheer up, old boy, because I am perfectly certain that everything is going to come right, and more quickly than you have any idea of."

She spoke the last words with meaning, and Basil looked at her, trying to read her face.

"Have you got something at the back of your mind, sweetheart?" he asked.

She nodded. She could not help it.

"There is something," she said—"a little something. I cannot tell you now, because it is not my secret, but wait and see. You will know more before long. For my part, I feel more happy and hopeful than I have been since our engagement."

For a moment he caught something of her gaiety. He lifted his glass, and drank. "To the future," he said, but the momentary animation flickered out, and it was a silent and sorrowful young man who kissed her farewell about half-past nine, at the corner of the street in which was the establishment for young ladies of the Demoiselles de Custine-Seraphin.

CHAPTER V

Gregory arrived at his hotel in the Latin Quarter about ten. Loneliness oppressed him, and he went to the couple of attics upon the top floor tenanted by himself and Deschamps. He hoped that the latter was in, and in a better mood. He wanted an explanation from him, and he was haunted by some half-formed fear that the Frenchman knew of some calamity that might be about to overtake them—that something had gone wrong, perhaps, with the great invention, or that their positions at the Société Générale Electrique were jeopardised.

There was no one in Deschamps' room as he switched on the electric light, so he crossed the landing and entered his own.

This room also was untenanted, but the light was full on. He started, for it could not have been turned on by him, and electric lights burning at unnecessary hours were viewed with great disfavour and the subsequent result in the monthly bill by the hotel proprietor. Almost immediately, however, he understood, for a note in Deschamps' handwriting, and addressed to him, lay upon the table.

He picked it up, and tore open the flimsy envelope, his hand trembling as he did so.

For some reason or other he felt strangely excited, and he experienced the feeling that something is about to happen which comes to everyone at certain times. The note was quite short. It stated that Deschamps had gone again to the Rue Petite Louise to visit the Carnet brothers, and told Basil, in terms that were imperative, to proceed there immediately upon his return. That there might be no doubt whatever of Deschamps' meaning, the letter concluded by saying, "The matter is most urgent. I can say no more, but come."

As Basil walked the considerable distance towards the woods quarter, he was ill at ease and also in a bad temper. It was impossible to disregard such a summons, but he saw no use nor meaning in it, while it seemed to him almost an impoliteness to trouble the kindly entertainers of the night before so soon again. He found his way to the long, narrow street of the wood-sheds and wood-workers without much difficulty, only once having to ask the way. As before, the street was ill-lit, and perfectly quiet, though this time he could see it much more plainly owing to the absence of fog and the light of a watery moon. He entered the little passage, and rapped on the counter. Almost immediately that he had done so the door behind flew open and Brother Charles came out.

The little man was apparently delighted to see him. He was cordiality itself.

"Monsieur Deschamps is within," he said. "Enter, monsieur. We have been expecting you."

Greatly wondering what this might mean, Basil Gregory passed through into the workshop, where he found Edouard Carnet and Deschamps sitting by the fire.

On this occasion one of the principal workbenches had been cleared of lumber, and a white cloth was spread upon it, with a salad and boned chickens from some neighbouring restaurant, flanked by several bottles of that execrable sweet champagne beloved by the unsophisticated Parisian at times of festival—the Parisian being at once the most accomplished gourmet, and the worst judge in Europe of sparkling wines.

Deschamps, who rose with his hosts as Basil entered, was no longer surly or depressed. On the contrary, Gregory saw at once that he was in a state of intense excitement. There was a high colour upon his swarthy face, and the big black eyes were glittering.

In fact, there was an unusual atmosphere of excitement about everyone present in the workshop, and insensibly, in the first few moments even, it began to communicate itself to the Englishman.

"We were waiting for you to begin supper," said Brother Edouard in his twittering voice. "Afterwards we will tell you—what we have to tell."

Basil was not hungry, but he sat down with the others. Both Deschamps and the Carnets ate quickly and said very little. It was as though they wished to be done with the meal, but when the first bottle of champagne was opened and the sweet wine creamed in the glasses Brother Charles rose and lifted his glass on high. "To the success of the greatest scheme that human genius ever evolved!" he piped. "To the ruin and overthrow of that vast and evil power whose slaves and victims we have been!" With a sudden gesture, he drained his glass and flung it on the floor, where it crashed into a hundred pieces.

Then he stood there trembling, his bird-like face twisted into a grotesque mask of hatred, which was reflected by his brother.

Gregory looked at one and the other with amazement and then turned to Deschamps. He saw that the latter's face was more deeply flushed than before, the whole expression was one of quivering eagerness and almost ferocious hope. Gregory leant back in his chair and very deliberately lit a cigarette.

"I do not want to be unduly inquisitive," he said, in a quiet and measured voice, "but if one of you gentlemen would kindly give me the slightest inkling of what you are talking about, and why you are all so excited, then perhaps I shall feel a little less bewildered than I do at the moment."

At this Deschamps broke into a torrent of words.

"My friend," he said, "our troubles are at an end! As Monsieur Charles has just said, one of the most stupendous schemes that has ever entered the human brain has come to me. By its means we shall all become fabulously wealthy in a short time if all goes well."

Basil was staring at his friend, wondering whether he had taken leave of his senses, when Charles Carnet interposed. "We shall not *all* become wealthy," he said. "Edouard and I have enough; we want no more. You will become wealthy, and we shall have our revenge."

"I am listening," said Gregory rather stolidly.

As if by common consent the other three rose from the table. "Come to the fire," Deschamps said, speaking now in a low voice, "and you shall hear everything."

They sat round the fire very close together, and, looking round as if to be quite certain that there was no one lurking in the recesses of the workshop, Deschamps began:

"*Mon ami,*" he said, putting his hand upon Basil's arm, "we are going to take a journey, you and I."

"A journey?" Gregory said.

"To Monte Carlo," Deschamps replied.

Then there was a silence; Basil felt his brain whirling. "What do you mean?" he said at length.

"I mean this," Deschamps answered, "that fortune is within our grip at last, that we can now make as much money as we like, enough to conduct all our experiments and get out perfect models of our invention to place before the world. I will explain."

He threw away the cigarette which he had been smoking and began to outline a plan so novel, a conspiracy so absolutely without precedent in the history of the world, that his three listeners remained spell-bound.

"Chance, and chance alone," he began, "has placed the opportunity for the most sensational coup of modern times in our hands. In the first place, chance—the Spirit of Fortune, or what you will—led us to this room in which we are sitting. The Messieurs Carnet, as you know, have for years been employed in making roulette wheels for the Casino at Monte Carlo. As you have also heard, they have resolved to give up their occupation. The tragedy which has saddened their lives has been directly due to the existence of the great gambling establishment. Both our friends would give anything to be revenged upon the organisation which has wrecked their hopes, and owing to the existence of which their so beloved nephew met his untimely death."

A low mutter of assent broke from both the little Frenchmen.

"Very well, then," Deschamps continued, "you have wondered at my abstraction during the last twenty-four hours. I could not speak to you. I was absorbed. I hardly heard anything you said. The whole forces of my intellect were focussed upon one thought, one aim. The germ of an idea came to me. It was like a lightning flash, illuminating with sudden splendour the dark skies of night. The flash came and went, but the germ of the idea remained behind. Since then I have been working unceasingly at it, and now I believe I have it perfected. You, yourself, my dear friend, will be able to seize on any flaw, to improve upon my original idea.

Very well, then; I came to our friends here, and told them that I believed I could, if I would, deal the Administration of Monte Carlo an almost fatal blow. It was, I explained to them, by means of science, and more especially of your and my new invention, that this could be done. I pointed out to them that it would require their co-operation. I think I may say"—here he looked interrogatively at the Carnets—"that directly I made my proposal they agreed."

"We welcomed it with joy," said Brother Edouard instantly. "To us also it came as a lightning flash, illuminating the dark and showing the word 'Revenge' in letters of fire upon the horizon!"

Basil leant forward, deeply interested. As yet he had not the slightest idea of what was coming. Nevertheless, he was so impressed by Deschamps' firm and confident manner that hope was beginning to rise high within him, and an excitement to which he had been a stranger for many days, began to flow over him like a tide.

Moreover, he knew Deschamps so well that he was certain that this was no vision. The Frenchman was a Southerner, it is true, given to pictorial flights of fancy in many ways. But when he began to speak of any matter connected with science or their invention, he never made the slightest overstatement. Science was his life and his religion.

"As yet," Deschamps said, "Monsieur Edouard and Monsieur Charles know nothing of the actual means I propose to employ. I am going to divulge my plan in such a way that they, knowing nothing of electricity and its powers, will be able to understand my project in every detail. I shall not use any technicalities beyond what are absolutely necessary. But you, *mon ami*, will understand everything from the scientific point of view, and you will see how perfectly feasible and likely of success is what I propose to do."

He paused, and going to the table, poured out a little water into a glass and drank it off. He did not sit down again, but walked up and down a measured beat of four yards, talking with intense earnestness.

"You know, gentlemen," he said to the two wood-carvers, "what wireless telegraphy means?"

"But, yes," said Brother Charles, "have they not just installed the Marconi system in the Eiffel Tower? Of course, we know, but not, I think, more than any ordinary member of the public."

"Very well," said Deschamps. "Now I must tell you that Monsieur Gregory here and myself have for years been at work upon a system of transmitting messages without wires, which, we believe, and indeed are certain, surpasses the invention of Signor Marconi as a modern battleship surpasses an ancient wooden frigate. It is this system of ours that I propose to employ in the secret war against the Administration at Monte Carlo. By its means we shall be able to win an enormous sum of money at roulette. We shall be able to win exactly how much, and when, we please. Every detail is perfectly clear in my mind, and discovery is almost impossible with the precautions I shall take. You must remember that the capital of Monte Carlo is unlimited. You know nothing of the place, Basil?"

Gregory shook his head.

"Then, pardon a short digression," Deschamps continued, looking at the Carnets. "The gambling rooms of Monte Carlo pay the Prince of Monaco a yearly subsidy of eighty thousand pounds for permission to carry on their business in his territory. There are no rates and taxes in Monte Carlo, the Casino pays them all. Education is free. The Casino itself is a glittering white palace upon the edge of the Mediterranean, erected at an enormous cost, and decorated with the most lavish splendour. Few kings have such vast halls and salons in their palaces as those in the temple of the Goddess of Chance. The Casino is free to all the world, though, of course, the Administration reserves the right of declining admission. The gardens that surround this palace are the most beautiful in the world. Sometimes, as if by touch of an enchanter's wand, the thousand gardeners steal out in the night, and in the morning vast parterres of flowers, which had been all red and gold as the sun sank, are changed to blue and white. In addition to this—and the expenses of the Principality are incalculable—the company pays a revenue to its shareholders of over twenty-five million francs!"

Basil had been listening with absorbed interest. He started now. "Twenty-five million francs!" he said, in an awed voice. "Clear profit after those colossal expenses? A million English pounds!"

"Exactly," Deschamps returned, "and I have told you this so that you can see that the resources of the company are practically unlimited. The amount of their funds no one knows, but many a national bank could not equal it. So you see, the authorities are pledged for the sake of their own continuance to pay any player his winnings, however enormous they may be. There have been several cases of players quite recently winning sums of two and a half million francs—a hundred thousand pounds of your English money. But we"—here his voice for the first time began to tremble with excitement—"we can win whatever we please! And now to the way in which it is to be done."

Deschamps stopped short in his walk up and down. He leant against the work-table upon which were the remains of the supper.

The eyes of the other three were fixed upon him with an intense regard.

"You understand," he said to Basil, "the principle of roulette, do you not?"

"Roughly," Basil answered; "the little ivory ball about the size of a large marble is spun as you spun it the other night, and falls into a numbered slot. The people who have placed their money upon a square of the table with a number corresponding to that of the slot into which the ball falls are the winners of varying amounts."

"That is more or less it," Deschamps replied. "I am not concerned at the moment with anything but the bare mechanical operation. The whirling of the wheel at the bottom, the opposite course of the ball, and the triangular silver stars which break it, all make it a pure matter of chance into which apartment upon the wheel the ball is going to fall. It is obvious, therefore, that if by some means the player could determine into which slot the ball is to fall, he would have the bank at his mercy."

"Precisely," Basil said.

"Very well, then. It is a means by which this may be attained that I have discovered. Of course, you, as an electrical engineer, can easily see that a roulette wheel might easily be constructed by the bank by which it could control the falling of the ball and so prevent players who had backed a particular number from winning. This has often been done by dishonest people who run private gambling hells. Upon the surface everything appears all right, but, of course, an expert examination would very speedily result in the discovery of the secret mechanism—generally, by the way, electrical. Wires can be hidden in the leg of the table upon which the wheel stands, and controlled by the foot of the croupier who spins it. But never before—and I wish you to keep this point most carefully in mind—has it been possible for the player to control the wheel in action without the connivance of the croupier or the bank. Now listen." He began to address himself now more particularly to the Carnet Frères.

"The first detail in my plan is that the little ivory ball, while remaining to all appearance a solid ball of ivory, is not really so. It will contain a core or heart of steel. The very finest workmanship alone could accomplish this without any possibility of detection. I assume—am I right in assuming?—that our friends, Messieurs Charles and Edouard, could make a ball or balls of this description."

The two little men, who had been listening with rigid attention, spoke to one another rapidly for a moment or two, using technical terms which the others could not understand.

Then Brother Charles looked up. "We can do it," he said proudly. "It will be difficult, very difficult. First of all, there is the weight to be considered, for the ball must not exceed a normal weight. Then there must be a special quality of ivory, and work in turning and hollowing so extraordinarily fine and delicate that perhaps only one of the Indian or Chinese carvers could do it so that the operation showed no trace. I am certain that no one in France but myself and my brother are capable of this feat, but you may rest content—it is not beyond our powers!"

The little man concluded with quiet pride, and Deschamps showed unmistakable relief.

"I was certain of it," he said, "but, naturally, I had some little anxiety. Everything, in the first instance, depends upon that."

"We then have our prepared ball or balls—for a whole set must be made. The next point is the peculiar construction of the rotating wheel upon which the slots are fixed. Then, you, Basil, will immediately understand, but I must explain it carefully to our friends, they will have to work under my instructions, and with material which I supply. The prepared wheel will be constructed quite differently from the ordinary ones, though it will look exactly the same, when painted with the numbers. Each slot, messieurs, will be constructed of metal varying very slightly in composition. To all outward appearance the metal will be just the ordinary tin amalgam generally employed. In reality, as far as the metal goes, each slot will have, so to speak, a personality of its own—a certain power of receptivity of certain influences which no other slot has."

He stopped for a moment, and suddenly Basil Gregory rose from his chair, and gave a great shout of excitement. A glimmering, a faint glimmering, of the stupendous idea had come to him, and he trembled all over with excitement.

The two little men were no less excited than he, though as yet they were in the dark.

Deschamps made a movement with his hand, Basil sat down again, and the Frenchman went on speaking.

"My colleague here," he said, "is already beginning to grasp the idea. In a very few more words you will understand it also. I mentioned wireless telegraphy to you just now. I also told you that my friend and I had improved enormously upon the present system, though, owing to lack of money, we have never been able as yet to place our invention upon the market or get it recognised, while if we took it to quarters where it would be appreciated and understood, we should be robbed of nearly all the profits, as has happened with many another inventor.

"Well, then, messieurs, the invention of my friend and myself—I speak purposely in non-technical terms—makes it possible for the mysterious electrical power which sends messages over thousands of miles of space—the Hertzian waves in short—to penetrate through any amount of material resistance in the form of the walls of buildings, or barriers of any kind. Marconi has already accomplished something of this; we have perfected it. Now, in wireless telegraphy it is already possible to 'tune' sets of instruments so that the message sent at one end of the transmitter will only be received at the other by a similarly tuned receiver, this preventing the message being picked up by other receivers as it flies through space. I am about to apply this principle, greatly facilitated by our invention, to the slots of the roulette wheel. Each slot will be tuned separately from its fellow. Having got thus far, let me explain to you that, by means of the Hertzian waves, the operator will be able to turn a slot into a temporary magnet of low power at any moment he desires. That is to say, that when the prepared wheel is being used upon the tables at Monte Carlo, an operator with his instrument may be three or four hundred yards away in the upper room of a neighbouring hotel, or, if necessary, two miles away up upon the mountains of the Maritime Alps, and will be able to turn any slot he desires into a magnet for just as long a period as he wishes it to remain so. There will be no visible connection between the distant operator and the wheel. It is absolutely impossible that the people clustered round the wheel can know what is going on. The great secret, silent power of electricity will be at work, and yet entirely unsuspected and unknown."

He paused again, and triumph dawned upon his face as he saw that now not only did Basil Gregory thoroughly understand the plan, but that the brothers Carnet also had grasped the idea. Their faces were blazing with amazement, their bodies tense and rigid, there was no sound in the workshop but that of his own voice.

"The rest is easy to explain," he said. "If, say, at a given moment, the slot painted seven is converted into a low-power magnet directly the wheel begins to revolve, then, as a natural consequence, as soon as the velocity of the ball begins to die away, and the attractive power of the magnet, which slot number seven has become, proves greater than the impelling force of the ball, the ball which has a steel core will fall into slot number seven.

"You will observe, then, that the unseen operator any distance from the Casino is absolute master of the play at the particular table where the prepared wheel is.

"His confederate will play at this table. He and the operator will carry watches that are absolutely and utterly reliable, and which are synchronised to a hundredth second of time. A course of play is determined on. A sequence of certain numbers is agreed upon between the two. Let us say that the player enters the rooms at twelve o'clock in the morning and secures his place at the special table. At ten minutes past twelve to the instant it is agreed that number seven, let us say, is to receive the force of the Hertzian waves for a certain definite period. As a usual thing, so rapid is the paying out and gathering in of money at the tables at Monte Carlo, the wheel is spun every minute and a half. Of course, if the stakes are very high, or if there is a dispute, a coup may take a little longer. That, however, is a fair working average. For a little less than a minute and a half, then, from the time agreed upon, i.e., ten minutes past twelve, seven will remain a magnet. For that particular spin seven must infallibly prove the winner. The thing can be repeated over and over again."

"It is marvellous!" the brothers shouted out in chorus. "It will be impossible to detect. Monsieur, you are the greatest mechanical genius the world has ever seen!"

It was a great moment for Emile Deschamps. All the theatrical instincts so deeply implanted within him were gratified. To watch the faces of his audience, to see the dawn of understanding and admiration as he talked, had been to him like cool water to one in the desert.

He stood still now, one hand upon his heart, and bowed. He had no thought of mockery, the gesture was perfectly spontaneous and sincere. He turned to Basil.

"And you, my friend, what do you think of it?" he asked.

Basil started. He had been thinking furiously, and the question came unexpectedly.

"It is, of course, extremely brilliant," he said. "Naturally I can see that even more readily than our friends here. I don't believe any brain but yours, Emile, would ever have thought of it. Properly worked, and there are a good many details I should like to discuss with you, it's almost certain the scheme will succeed. But— —"

"Ah," Deschamps burst in, "the usual English reservation! The invariable 'but' of caution! What is it now, you cold-blooded islander?"

"Oh, it is not caution," Basil answered. "Haven't I just told you that the thing must succeed with a few modifications upon your original idea? It is the morality of the thing I am thinking of."

Deschamps had sat down. He jumped up now like a Jack-in-the-box. "*Tiens!*" he cried. "Morality? Morality?"

"I thought you had forgotten the meaning of the word," Basil answered dryly. "It seems to me—I only offer the opinion for what it is worth—that while this little plan is about as alluring a proposition as I ever heard, one of the most elementary problems of life has been quite lost sight of. We are going to steal—to put it quite frankly. It is an iridium-pointed, hot-pressed, wire-wove, jewelled-in-every-hole sort of steal, I know, but it is a steal all the same, isn't it? I am open to conviction, of course, and, by the way, if anything goes wrong, conviction is just what will occur. We have a little poem in England which sums up the question in a nutshell—

He who prigs what isn't his'n,
When he's cotched will go to prison;

or, to put it in simpler form still, 'the penalty for abstracting quids by electricity will be quod'—you are a Latin scholar, I believe, Emile?"

The Frenchman made an impatient and angry gesture of his hands.

"There is no time for *blague*," he said, "with your quids and your quods. I know nothing of your piggish English play upon words. Of course, if it is the fear of discovery that deters you, and the possibilities of arrest, well——"

He did not conclude, but shrugged his shoulders, and puffed out his lips with a peculiarly French contempt.

Basil was quite unmoved. "It is not that," he said, "as you know very well, Emile. I would risk anything upon any chance. Our lives at the present moment are very like two puddings in a fog. Prison could not be much worse. But I do not quite see how one is going to reconcile this marvellously ingenious plan of yours with ordinary morals. There have been lots of times when you and I have wanted a bottle of wine or a packet of cigarettes very badly, and hadn't the money to pay for them. If I had proposed to you to take a bottle of chambertin while the wine-merchant was not looking—well!"

The two little Frenchmen had been listening with keen attention to this dialogue. Basil's English irony had been lost upon them, but they understood the main lines of his objections well enough.

It was Brother Edouard who came to the rescue.

"Permit me to say a word," he interrupted in his gentle, high-pitched voice. "The cases of robbing a wine-merchant and the Administration of Monte Carlo have not the slightest analogy. Your premises are false, Monsieur Gregoire. This organisation at Monte Carlo is simply a soulless machine for the making of money by exploiting one of the baser passions of men. I and my brother—I freely confess it—have been parts of that machine for years. But you know the sad event"—his voice trembled a little—"which opened our eyes. We said to each other, 'If our hopes in life have all been utterly swept away in an instant by the Casino at Monte Carlo, how many other homes have been ruined, young lives sacrificed, prospects blighted?' A soldier who assists to exterminate, or, at any rate, to harass and injure a dangerous and unfriendly tribe of savages is generally looked upon as doing a fine and meritorious thing. Nor does he disdain to take the pay of his country for so doing. You and Monsieur Deschamps will be in exactly the same case. You will be seriously injuring the Casino. It may be that when the idea is developed roulette will become impossible, though that is only a side issue, and also—here you must listen to me carefully—you are not proposing to obtain a large sum of money for the mere gratification of low pleasures, to acquire a soulless ease and comfort. You have invented something which will be of the highest benefit to mankind. Want of fortune alone prevents you conferring that benefit upon the world. As inventors, it is your duty—at least, so it appears to me—to take advantage of the opportunity which the genius of Monsieur Deschamps has provided. No one will be hurt except people who can well afford to suffer."

His voice had gathered strength as he went on, and as he concluded there was an almost prophetic note in it, a gravity and seriousness of conviction which had an instant effect upon Basil Gregory's wavering mind.

He thought for a minute, and then looked up.

"So be it," he said. "You have convinced me, though I will say I was ready enough to be convinced. We will try it. Like all other gamblers, we will risk everything upon a single throw."

As if by common consent, they all rose to their feet.

"And now," said Brother Charles, who had hitherto been silent, "let us form ourselves into a committee of ways and means."

Deschamps' face grew pale. "*Mon Dieu!*" he cried, "fool that I am! I have been carried away by the splendour of the prospect, and have forgotten the most essential fact of all. Our friends here"—he was speaking to Basil—"can prepare the wheel with my assistance. But how about the apparatus, which, as you know, is costly enough for ordinary purposes? The particular apparatus I shall want with all our own modifications and specialities will cost about five thousand francs. And then there is the getting to Monte Carlo, the putting up at an expensive hotel to avoid suspicion—for the Administration has its spies and detectives everywhere. It may be necessary to bribe, a thousand emergencies may occur, which only money can overcome."

He dived one hand into the pocket of his trousers, and withdrew four coins. He flung them on the floor with a curse.

"Three francs fifty!" he cried; "three francs fifty! Basil, I am a fool and a dreamer! You can preserve your morality unspotted, after all!"

Basil looked blankly at his friend, who was now limp with an almost ferocious dejection and self-contempt. He nodded slowly.

"Same old thing," he said; "we ought to have expected it. We are stumped, old chap, for want of three or four hundred pounds."

An odd hissing noise, like the escape of steam from a very small pipe, recalled him to his surroundings. The brothers Carnet were regarding the two young men with pity. "Ah!" said Brother Charles, almost wringing his hands, "What fools these men of genius are, Edouard! Messieurs! Messieurs! my brother and I will, of course, provide the funds. Haven't we already told you that we are quite well-to-do for people in our position? You will draw on us for any money you may require. Nor must you spare the francs. This is a great affair, conduct it greatly, and you will earn our undying gratitude."

Once more the volatile Deschamps was transformed from limp dejection to painful excitability. He leapt at both the little men, and embraced each in turn. He called down blessings upon their heads, and then, in an instant, assumed the manner of a calm business-like man.

He took a fountain-pen and an envelope from his pocket.

"You will, of course, take whatever proportion of our winnings you think fit, gentlemen," he said, "and as far as the amount of the winnings is concerned, you have only to say the word. It will be as well to make a note of the terms at once, and we will have a proper agreement drawn out."

The Carnets looked at Basil Gregory as much as to say, "What a hopeless person this Southerner is!" Basil, far quicker than Deschamps to understand the odd little men, changed the subject at once. "Never mind about that now, Emile," he said. "Our friends have very kindly offered to advance the money necessary for the great coup. We had now better go into other details, so as not to lose time. Financial affairs can be arranged later."

Deschamps nodded. "Very well, then," he said, "let us recapitulate what is absolutely necessary to be done, immediately. In the first place, you and I must give up our positions at the Société Générale."

Basil started at this. "Is that really necessary?" he asked. "Couldn't we get leave?"

Deschamps shook his head. "I feel almost sure they won't give us leave," he said. "We are only members of the rank and file, remember. But 'nothing venture, nothing have,'—we must resign."

"Very well," Basil replied, "we will give them notice to-morrow." But as he said it he had a curious heart-pang as he thought of Ethel, and that, if anything went wrong, he must resign for ever any hopes of calling her his own.

"Now, about experiments and the construction of the apparatus," Deschamps continued. "We must have a workshop, to begin with."

"This is at your service," the brothers said eagerly.

Deschamps bowed. "A thousand thanks," he said. "Nothing could be better fitted for the purpose. Here we shall be absolutely secret. You have a forge and many appliances which will be useful. To-morrow I must buy other machinery and certain tools. Fortunately you have the electric light here, and I can tap one of the plugs for all the current that I shall require for experimental purposes."

Basil snapped his fingers as if an idea had just come to him. "By Jove, Emile!" he said, "how on earth shall we manage at Monte Carlo? We cannot work with batteries. First of all, we could never get them into the hotel without being seen, and even if we did, we shouldn't have enough power."

"You don't know the Principality," Emile answered. "All the hotels have the completest installation of electric light possible. It will be the simplest thing to tap one of the mains and connect it with our new portable transformer. We can get exactly what current we require."

"Good," Basil said, realising how deeply his friend had gone into the technical side of the great coup.

Edouard Carnet spoke. "If you will come here to-morrow at midday," he said, "having already resigned your posts at the Société Générale, I will have drawn a sufficient sum of money from the bank to enable you to make all necessary purchases. Then we can go ahead as fast as we like."

"But don't forget this, brother," Charles Carnet interposed, "our new wheels must be dispatched to Monaco. As a matter of fact, they are expecting them immediately, but a telegram saying that we require another fortnight will put that right. We have had to take a little extra time before now, during the past years. A fortnight, however, is as much grace as we shall be able to get and preserve our friendly relations with the Administration. Will you be able to do all that is necessary in the construction of the apparatus within a fortnight?"

"It will be quick work," Deschamps replied, "but it can be done. My friend and myself can construct the necessary apparatus for sending the waves, and we can also, with your co-operation, prepare the wheel and tune the slots for the reception of the vibrations."

Then Basil spoke. "Look here, Emile," he said, "a thought strikes me. Of course, I don't know anything about the Casino, and I have never been to the South of France, but won't it look strangely suspicious if we win day by day at the same table? Won't they change the wheel?"

"That is exactly what they will do, monsieur," Edouard Carnet replied to him. "Of course, when a man wins a large sum at one table he always goes to the same table to play. It is his lucky table. But there was a case some years ago when a little syndicate of players—by means of the most careful calculations—noticed that the wheel of the table where they made their game had a slight bias. They traded on the fact for several days, and won an enormous sum of money. It was one of our wheels, but there must have been a flaw in the wood, or we had not allowed for the expansion of the metal, owing to the greater heat of the South. At any rate, as a result, the wheels have been constantly changed ever since."

"Then, how can we carry out our plan?" Basil asked.

"The wheels are not taken away entirely," Edouard went on; "they are simply changed from table to table. The prepared wheel will have some distinguishing mark by which you will know it. We must think that out; it must be some very slight thing—a knot in the wood, a mere scratch on the outside, would do."

A dry little chuckle came from Brother Charles.

"We are getting on! We are getting on!" he said, with a grotesque mirth. "My brother, what is to prevent us preparing three wheels? They should be 'tuned'—as Monsieur Deschamps calls it—exactly alike. Each will be marked in some way, so that our friends can distinguish them from the unprepared wheels. There are twelve roulette wheels in all used in the Salle des Jeux."

"*Bien!*" Edouard replied; "your brain moves quickly. By this means our friends will be able to move from table to table as they wish."

"And I would suggest," Deschamps broke in, "that we do not play for more than a week in all. In a week's time we shall be able to win an enormous sum of money, without unduly exciting suspicion. Great runs of luck, I have observed, generally last for about seven or eight days. If, as Monsieur Charles suggests, we move from table to table, a week should be sufficient. We can go away with enormous sums, and no one will be any the wiser."

"And another thing," Edouard Carnet said, "which of you is going to be the actual operator of the telegraphic instrument, and which the player at the tables?"

"Oh, I'd much better play," Deschamps answered, "and Basil work the instrument."

Both the Carnets shook their heads at this.

"No," they said together, "that will be unwise. Monsieur Gregoire is typically English. It is always best for a foreigner to make these great coups. Moreover, the luck of the English and the Americans is proverbial. Monsieur Gregoire must be thought an English millionaire. No one thinks it strange when a millionaire wins another million! But, to safeguard the future, it would be as well that monsieur were disguised."

Basil shook his head. "Disguised!" he cried. "Oh, I don't like that idea at all!"

"It is necessary," Edouard Carnet said firmly; "but all that you have to do, monsieur, is to shave off that blonde moustache, darken your skin a little, and wear pince-nez. It is only ordinary caution, after all. When you return with the spoils of war and grow your moustache again, nobody will ever connect you with the winner of millions upon the Côte d'Azur."

"And I have another idea," twittered Brother Charles, his little face beaming with joy. "Monsieur Deschamps shall go to Monte Carlo as the valet of Monsieur Gregoire. It will all seem so natural—the assiduous valet, the heavy luggage, which the man-servant must guard! You see it?"

The situation struck Basil as humorous. He threw back his head and laughed aloud. "Emile," he said.

Deschamps entered into the spirit of the thing. "*Bien*, monsieur," he answered.

"Sit down at the table and teach me the rules of the game of roulette!"

PART II

CHAPTER VI

Two men sat alone in a first-class compartment of the Riviera train-de-luxe.

The night before the most luxurious train in Europe had left the Gare de Lyon at Paris. The night had been bitterly cold, and as the vast machine swung out of the station all the suburbs of Paris and, indeed, the plains of mid-France, were seen through the dark windows of the corridors to be covered with a white sprinkling of snow.

A special carriage was reserved for a Monsieur Montoyer and his valet, and the two persons mentioned upon the ticket had spent the whole night in the luxurious cabin, with its beds and little tables, talking earnestly.

Monsieur Charles Edouard Montoyer was an athletic, burly looking young man, dressed in the height of French fashion, clean-shaved, dark-complexioned, and wearing gold-rimmed spectacles, which only partially concealed a pair of blue eyes which seemed oddly at variance with his otherwise Southern appearance. His hair also was a dead black, and in certain lights it had an almost metallic lustre.

The valet presented no very extraordinary appearance, except that he seemed markedly intelligent and alert. His black hair was closely cropped to a large and well-shaped head. His complexion was of the true Southern swarthy tint, glowing out below the skin, as it were. He wore a small black moustache, and the long first finger of his right hand was deeply stained with the juice of cigarettes.

Once, about an hour after the start, the valet went to the restaurant car, and brought back two bowls of soup, and a bottle of Pomard, explaining to the waiter who gave them that his master was very hungry and one tureen would be insufficient. But when the door of the sleeping-car was locked, the blinds looking on the corridor drawn down, the table set, and all the electric lights switched on, a spectator—had there been one there—would have seen with some surprise that master and man shared the meal equally. And perhaps he would have thought it a touching testimony of the theoretical equality of Republican France that master and man addressed each other by their Christian names.

In short, the great enterprise was begun, Basil and Emile, their apparatus made, their plan of campaign concluded, were roaring and crashing through France to the fairy-like shores of the Mediterranean.

It was now close upon nine o'clock in the morning. The blinds of the sleeping-car were still drawn upon the corridor side, but the two men were dressed. Their hand luggage was strapped and they were smoking cigarettes.

"In a moment more, Basil," said Emile, his voice trembling with excitement, "in a moment more you shall have your first vision of the South! I would not let you look before and, indeed, as we went through Avignon it was too dark to see much, but Marseilles—my beloved native city—is the Gate of the South. You will see little of it, as within an hour we shall be pulling out again for the Côte d'Azur, but you will see something; you will at least breathe the enchanted air!"

Deschamps' voice was most powerfully affected. For a moment he had forgotten the enterprise entirely. He was only consumed with an over-mastering eagerness that his dearest friend and partner should breathe with him that subtle, intoxicating air, and realise for the first time in his life what the South means.

There was a long grinding of the brakes, and the train stood still. Emile drew up the blinds, opened the door into the corridor, and led Basil to the end of the car. Then they stepped down to the low platform.

They had left Paris in sullen bitter winter weather. Here, early as it was, the sun was shining brilliantly in the cool, quiet station. Exactly facing them was a huge stall of flowers, masses of purple violets, delicate ivory-coloured roses from Grasse, the pale golden plumes of the mimosa.

But the air! the air was the thing! So warm and sweet it was, it came upon them with such a veritable caress, it so bathed them with golden light and sweet odours, that tears started into Deschamps' eyes, and Basil forgot his disguise.

"How wonderful! how wonderful!" he said in English, breathing like a man who had been stifled all his life.

And that was their first glimpse of the enchanted country to which they had come.

Through all the morning until mid-afternoon the train moved, slowly and sleepily now, through scenes of loveliness such as the Englishman, at any rate, had never dreamed of. Everywhere the Mediterranean gleamed like an immense sapphire, flecked here and there with white fire. The low cliffs of sandstone were crimson. The sky was an inverted bowl of glowing turquoise, and everywhere tall, feathery palms were silhouetted against it in brilliant green. And there were flowers, flowers everywhere! Every station with its familiar name was full of flowers—Grasse, Cannes, Nice, Villefranche—there were flowers everywhere; flowers, exotic trees, and great white hotels that gleamed jewel-like in terrace after terrace from the sea till they were lost in the high places of the Maritime Alps.

And then—at last—Monaco, a few tunnels cut in the cliffs, and the long, low station of Monte Carlo at last!

During the whole period of the slower journey along the seashore Basil Gregory's excitement had been gradually growing. He and Deschamps had talked but little, but both of them had been obsessed by the great idea that they were getting nearer and nearer to the world-famous theatre of their colossal enterprise.

Monte Carlo! Monte Carlo! The words had beaten themselves into a rythm in Basil's brain, a rythm in tune with the regular pulsing of the engine.

They were to stay at the Hôtel Malmaison, for the brothers Carnet had insisted that the two young men should lack nothing, and that Basil should appear to be a person of great wealth and consequence. There was to be no hole-and-corner business about the great coup. Suspicion was to be averted by every possible means. *"Il fait aller en regal,"* Brother Charles had insisted, and so it was to be. Rooms had been engaged in advance, a sitting-room and bedroom for Monsieur Charles Edouard Montoyer, and a bedroom for his valet. It had been stipulated, however, that the valet's bedroom should be at the very top storey of the hotel, as that personage suffered from asthma.

The Malmaison was only some four hundred yards from the station, and in consequence some three hundred from the Casino. They drove there in the waiting omnibus, however, and at five o'clock were installed in their rooms.

It was a little difficult to account for two large boxes among the luggage, of extraordinary heaviness, which were placed in the sitting-room of Monsieur Montoyer. But the ready Deschamps in his rôle of valet explained that monsieur was a great student, and always travelled with many books.

"I go now, *mon ami*" Emile said, "to my own room. All your clothes are unpacked. I must not stay here too long at present. I shall have to meet all the other servants and gossip with them, but I will come at seven to assist you to dress, and then we can make our plans."

Basil was left alone in the brightly furnished sitting-room. He looked down into a terraced garden, brilliant still with the declining rays of the sun. Somewhere near by a band of guitars was playing accompanied by voices as sweet and passionate as they.

He strolled up and down the room thinking deeply. But it was not of the fairyland in which he found himself, it was not of the glories he was soon to witness, it was not even of the great hazard he was to try—the bold and reckless bid for fortune. It was of Ethel he was thinking.

CHAPTER VII

About ten o'clock in the morning of the day on which Basil Gregory and Emile Deschamps had arrived at Monte Carlo, another train had pulled into the long low station on the Mediterranean shore.

This train was very different from the huge, luxurious machine that brought the adventurers to the City of Fortune earlier in the day. It was the ordinary slow train, the third class, not even a *rapide*, and only a few second-class carriages were included in its make-up. Moreover, it had taken two whole days, and nights in its journey from Paris, being everywhere shunted aside for the *rapides* and *trains de luxe* to pass through.

From this train of poorer people two English ladies, quietly dressed, and pale and stained with travel under none too pleasant conditions, had descended.

They were driven at once with their trunks to a modest *pension* in the Rue Grimaldi in Monaco, and spent some hours in sleep.

Ethel McMahon had told her lover in Paris that she had obtained a fortnight's leave of absence from her school, had saved a little money, and was about to take her mother to Switzerland for a change of air.

Basil had accepted the statement implicitly, glad to hear that the girl he loved was to have a short respite from her labours, and, for his own part, finding that the proposed holiday would coincide with his own absence from Paris, he said nothing of his plans. So it had been arranged, and the two lovers were mutually ignorant of each other's purposes and without the slightest idea that they were bound for the same destination. Mrs. McMahon had absolutely refused to allow Ethel to communicate a word of their project to Gregory, and the girl was all the more ready because by now she was thoroughly infected with her mother's enthusiasm, and was absolutely convinced in her own mind that they were to gain a small fortune at the tables.

How splendid it would be to come to Basil and to tell him that they could be married at once! That funds for the launching of the great invention were forthcoming, that all was to end as happily as some old song!

About six o'clock Ethel went into her mother's room. The rest had refreshed her. Her eyes were glowing with excitement, and with her long hair falling over her dressing-gown she seemed the personification of radiant hope.

"Now, what are we to do, mother?" she said excitedly. "How do you feel?"

The older woman was seated in the one arm-chair the little bedroom of the *pension* boasted, and was anxiously scrutinising a bundle of faded papers covered with figures and bold masculine handwriting.

"It is certain, Ethel!" she said. "I have been going through your father's figures for the hundredth time. I am sure it can't fail. You know he only invented this particular system just before he died, and we never had an opportunity to try it properly."

Ethel nodded. "I feel just as you do, mother, dear," she answered. "It *can't* fail. But what are we to do? Are you thoroughly rested?"

"I feel in better health," the old lady answered, "than I have felt for years. Excitement would keep me up if nothing else would, but, as it is, I have no trace of fatigue. What's the use of spending the evening in this dull *pension* with these third-rate people, for such of the guests as I have seen are rather a seedy-looking lot, and Madame de Bonville is just the ordinary Southern Frenchwoman who keeps a place of this sort? No! We will dress, have dinner, and take a cab to the Casino. There will be no difficulty about obtaining our tickets for this evening. We shall have to renew them each day, until we have been here for some time—if, indeed, it is necessary to remain here. After a week or two they give you a ticket for a month, but I don't suppose we shall need that."

"Then we are to begin to-night!" Ethel cried, a flush mounting in her cheeks and her voice ringing with anticipation.

The elder lady smiled. "We will not begin the system to-night," she answered. "That, I do think, would be unwise. We will take a louis or two and get a place at one of the tables, if we can, and just see what happens. I want you to get accustomed to a scene which will seem extraordinarily strange to you. We will take it that we are merely reconnoitring this evening, and begin serious play upon the morrow. Dinner is at half-past seven, so go and prepare yourself, my child, and then come and help me."

Ethel left the room and crossed the passage to her own, singing for sheer lightness of heart. Already the beauty of the South had caught hold of her, and such glimpses of it as she had seen only intensified her mood. In her innocence she had not the slightest misgiving. She would have laughed to scorn anyone who had told her that there was a chance of losing the little unexpected capital that had come to them from the lottery.

Dinner at the *pension de Bonville* was the ordinary polyglot affair. An English major—no regiment specified—some stolid Germans, three shrill-voiced American girls, and some nondescript and rather haggard looking young men made up the company. Doings at the Casino during the day were compared and discussed. The little cards, printed in red and black, which are provided by the Casino authorities for recording the play, and pricked each time the wheel is spun, were handed about, and in this atmosphere, so familiar to her in the past, old Mrs. McMahon seemed like a changed being. She talked with the rest, in English or fluent French; she was like some old war horse once more snuffling the breeze of battle, and Ethel was no less interested and entranced, though her knowledge of roulette—for none of the *pensionnaires* seemed to indulge in the more expensive *trente-et-quarante*—was purely theoretical.

After dinner the major gallantly offered to escort the ladies to the Casino and to obtain their tickets. Shortly afterwards, muffled in opera cloaks, for between eight and nine is often the coldest hour of the day on the Riviera, the three walked up the steep, winding way towards the Palace of Chance.

A full moon hung in the sky; everywhere were brilliant illuminations; the air as it proved was not at all cold upon this night, but soft and odorous of flowers.

The gardens of the Casino were like enchantment to Ethel McMahon. It was indeed a scene from the "Arabian Nights." The tall palms clicked faintly in the breeze with a sound like distant castanets. The electric lights shone down upon enormous beds of flowers which everywhere studded the lawns. Faint music was heard on every side, and gaudily painted and luxurious automobiles flitted noiselessly along the polished roadways.

Here was the great Hôtel de Paris, its long façade glowing with colour, full of the wealthiest people in the world, dining very differently from the way in which the major and his new friends had dined in the Rue Grimaldi. Beyond, on the other side of the square, were the gardens of the Métropole, and the glass Café de Paris at its side winked and glittered like a gigantic topaz.

"That, my dear," said Mrs. McMahon, pointing to a modest looking restaurant in an arcade, "that is Ciro's."

Ethel's sense of humour was tickled by the calm patronage of the information. She knew, of course, that she was looking upon the most famous restaurant in the whole world, but her mother's tone amused her.

And then, in a moment, she had no thought but one.

Before her was a magnificent building of white marble with many steps leading to a wide entrance, glistening against the background of dark sky, spangled with golden stars.

Mrs. McMahon clutched her daughter's arm. "There!" she said, almost in an awed whisper. "Now you see it for the first time. That is the Casino!"

For a moment all three were silent. The spirit of chance, the terrible fever of the gambler was in their blood, and even the tough old major, an *habitué* of every gambling hell in Europe, shared for a moment the emotion of his companions as they surveyed the supreme Temple of Chance.

They went up the steps, Ethel alert to everything she saw, and turned into a long office to the left, rather more like a small bank than anything else.

Two or three civil, quickly glancing Frenchmen, in black frock coats, were standing in this room before the counter. Ethel was conscious of a quick all-embracing scrutiny from three pairs of dark eyes, she heard her name spoken in French by one of the officials, and shortly afterwards two purple cards, bearing the mystic words:

"Cercle des Etrangers,
Valable pour un jour,"

and with their names written upon the back in thin clerkly script, were handed to them.

From there, into a vestibule where cloaks were exchanged for metal discs with a number upon them, and then in their evening frocks, but still wearing their hats, the two ladies passed with their cavalier into the Atrium.

The huge hall, with its galleries, marble columns and tesselated floor, its gleaming lights in the roof, and its little groups of people dotted here and there under the galleries or in the centre space, reminded Ethel of a dance she had once attended in England at the magnificent town hall of a great Northern city. Everyone was in evening dress, everyone talked animatedly, new arrivals kept constantly pouring in. But at one end of this enormous hall, where the huge marble pillars clustered more thickly, was a series of great swing doors of an abnormal height, doors which constantly opened noiselessly and closed again. And round the doors were innumerable officials in their long frock coats, standing there watching and waiting as the votaries of Chance pressed inwards to the very sanctum of the Temple.

Mrs. McMahon nodded. "Come, Ethel," she said in a voice that was positively hoarse with excitement, "the rooms are in there; let us go."

The two ladies walked up the long hall, presented their cards to an official who glanced at them and bowed, and then one of the great doors swung open and they entered. Although it was early yet, the rooms were fairly full.

Ethel found herself in an enormous salon of great height, and with a polished parquet floor. It resembled nothing so much as an immense ball-room in some royal palace. The walls were covered by huge pictures let into the gilded panelling, separated from each other by pilaster after pilaster of gold. The ceilings, also, where electric lights glowed brilliantly, were painted, and the general effect was one of almost overpowering magnificence. Beyond this huge salon she saw, under an immense archway, there was another and even larger one crossing it at right angles, and beyond that still another. The size and splendour of the place made her catch her breath and dazzled her eyes. "How wonderful!" she whispered to her mother.

Her next impression was that she was in some church! Despite the gorgeous decoration certainly not in the least ecclesiastical, the size and shape, the curious hush and silence that pervaded everything, helped the impression. There was only the very lowest murmur of conversation perceptible. Women in astonishingly gorgeous toilets, with gold purses hanging from their wrists by jewel-studded chains, moved slowly up and down the parquet floor with a rustling of skirts. The air was full of mingled perfume and suggested that odour of incense in a cathedral.

As all these impressions crowded into her mind, the girl's eyes became more used to the surroundings, and she saw, at intervals under the high dome-like roof, long tables were set, each one as long as two billiard tables. There were four of them in this first salon, and many more stretched away in the vista of brilliance.

The air was quite clear, nobody was smoking, and she could see everything very distinctly.

Around each table was a thick cluster of people, men and women, almost entirely hiding it from view.

She turned to the table nearest her.

Around it, without any intervals, people were sitting in chairs. Behind them stood other people, at some tables two deep. Above the tables were suspended huge lamps with green shades—like the lights over a billiard table, though not so brilliant.

"Why, they are oil lamps!" Ethel said in a low voice to her mother. "How strange and antiquated!"

Mrs. McMahon smiled.

"If they had electric lights immediately over the tables," she said, "or even gas, some of the gangs of bad characters who infest Monte Carlo would find means to cut the pipes or wires, and in the confusion anybody could take what money he pleased." She clutched her daughter's arm tightly. "Child," she said, in an impressive voice, "at any one of these tables at the present moment, lying about, unprotected, in notes and gold, there is at least fifty thousand pounds!"

At that moment the major drew their attention to the fact that at a table immediately ahead of them there was a little stir and movement.

A very tall and handsome young man had risen from his chair. His face was a little flushed and his eyes sparkled, while he tried in vain to conceal the smile of pleasure and excitement upon his lips. Several of the other people at this table, who all appeared to know him, rose also and began to congratulate him in low voices.

"That is the Archduke Theodore," the major said in a husky whisper. "He is a cousin of the Tsar. For the last week he has been winning enormous sums, and apparently he has done so again to-night. His pockets are simply bulging with notes!"

Mrs. McMahon looked significantly at Ethel. Then she saw her chance. "Come," she said, "we can sit down at this table. This is a very fortunate chance." They went to the table and found two chairs unoccupied, slipping into them quickly in the momentary diversion created by the Archduke's success, and for the first time Ethel McMahon sat actually a guest of the unknown goddess of Fortune, and about to woo her.

To the girl's unaccustomed eyes the scene was bewilderingly strange. The long expanse of green baize cloth stretched away on either side of her. It was marked with numbered squares and triangles, while at one end were two huge diamonds of red and black in either corner. She faced a row of people, men and women in correct evening costume, save that the women, like herself, wore the large hats which are *de rigueur* in the Casino. Jewels gleamed bewilderingly almost everywhere. Exactly opposite her was a woman who was simply plastered with diamonds, and yet next this gorgeous vision with the painted face and laughing eyes, with a king's ransom round her throat and in her hair, sat an elderly yellow-faced woman in a black dress and without a single ornament—more quietly and even shabbily dressed than Mrs. McMahon herself. There were two fresh-faced English boys, who looked like soldiers, there was an enormous black-bearded Bulgarian, with eyes like black velvet and hands like fat claws.

And all these people, on the green baize before them, had wads of notes or piles of gold, save only the old lady, before whom were only a few five-franc pieces—the minimum stake allowed at Monte Carlo.

And on the numbers themselves money was already beginning to be placed from every part of the table. Sometimes the people pushed it themselves on the chosen numbers, sometimes, when they were too far away, they gave it to one of the silent croupiers who sat round among the people and pushed the coins to the destined spot with their long india-rubber-tipped rakes.

Dividing the long table in the centre was the wheel itself, and the croupier in charge of it was already fingering the ivory ball. Behind him, on a higher seat, sat the official in charge of all the others engaged at this table, and from his lips came the occasional croak of the famous "*Faites vos jeux, messieurs: faites vos jeux.*"

Ethel had three golden louis in her purse. It was all the money that they had brought with them.

Her mother had told her that beginners nearly always won the first time they played—a very common superstition among gamblers, and one which, for some reason or other, seems to be amply justified.

"What shall I do, mother?"

"Do whatever you like," Mrs. McMahon answered quickly. "I mustn't influence you or it will spoil the luck."

Ethel hesitated, and as she did so the croupier swung the capstan and spun the ball.

A low, humming whirr broke the silence.

"Quick! quick!" whispered Mrs. McMahon, "make your stake or it will be too late."

Hardly knowing what she did, Ethel pushed her three louis on to the green cloth, and as she did so the ball began to rattle on the diamond-shaped pieces of silver at the side of the bowl, and the croupier called out sharply, "*Rien ne va plus,*" announcing that no more stakes could be put upon the table.

Ethel had pushed her three golden louis exactly upon the edge of the line which divided six numbers, from 13 to 18, unconsciously played what is called a *transversale simple.*

If any of these six numbers turned up she would win five times her original stake. And now—it all passed in a few seconds—the ball was rattling among the compartments, clicking like a pair of castanets. There was a final click as it fell into the slot, the croupier put out his finger and stopped the capstan, announcing the number—"*Rouge—dix-huit!*"

Red had turned up, but with that Ethel had no concern as she had not backed the colour, but 18 had won, though for a moment she did not realise it.

Then followed what to her was an extraordinary scene. The long rakes of the croupiers shot out from every part of the table, threading their way in and out among the masses of gold, silver and bank notes with extraordinary rapidity and the most delicate manipulation.

A small fortune was swiftly swept away into the bank until the table was comparatively bare. It was all done with the precision of a machine, without a single mistake, and hardly was it completed when the stakes of those who had won were being added to in a golden shower.

It takes a croupier at Monte Carlo a whole year to learn his business, but when he has learnt it no juggler upon the stage can provide a more startling exhibition. Coins flew from rapidly moving hands in a continuous stream, as if liquid gold was being squirted from a hose. No single coin rolled off its appointed square, but fell flat and motionless within an inch of the stake at which it was aimed. And now the rakes were pushing money towards the fortunate, not gathering it in any more, and, almost ere eager or indifferent hands had gathered up what Fortune had sent them, stakes were again being spread over the board for the next coup. To Ethel, who had not in the least known what had happened, there suddenly came a shower of gold falling just before her upon her original three louis.

She stared at it bewildered, and the big Bulgarian opposite smiled at her ignorance.

Not so Mrs. McMahon. "That is yours, Ethel," she said; "that is yours. You've won, after all." And as if in a dream the girl drew the glittering pile towards her. Fifteen louis, and her own three coins back again! Fifteen louis! More than thirteen English pounds—come to her as if by magic in less than a minute; her own, her very own to do as she liked with.

"I can't believe it!" she whispered to her mother. "It can't be true—all this—more than a quarter's salary in a minute!"

Old Mrs. McMahon was trembling with excitement, but there was triumph in her voice.

"My dear," she said, in those very tones of calm superiority which she had used when the lottery ticket had at last turned up trumps, "this is nothing. What did I tell you!"

"What shall I do now?" was Ethel's only answer. "Perhaps it would be better to do nothing."

Mrs. McMahon caught at the word with the true gambler's instinct. "My dear," she said, "put one of those louis upon zero."

There was a croupier three or four seats away from the girl. She leant forward, being now a little more accustomed to what she was doing, "*Zero, s'il vous plait, monsieur,*" she said, tossing the coin to him.

"*En plein, mademoiselle?*" he asked.

Ethel turned to her mother. "What does he mean?" she said. Mrs. McMahon interposed. "*Oui, en plein,*" she replied to the man. "You see, Ethel, it is rather unusual to stake a coin upon a single number, because you have thirty-five chances against you. Most people do what you did just now—cover several numbers and be content with smaller winnings. But you said 'nothing,' and it may be an omen."

Again the ball spun, and now, in full consciousness of what was happening, Ethel knew excitement so fierce and keen, so utterly overpowering and absorbing, that it burned within her like a flame, and frightened her by its intensity.

Her coin was the only one upon zero, which is the bank's number, for when it turns up all the stakes upon the board are taken by the bank, except those placed upon red or black, or the other even chances.

Dame Fortune was very kind to-night, for with a slight emphasis the croupier at the wheel called out "Zero," and several people within her vicinity turned to look with envy or amusement, as the case might be, at the beautiful girl who had alone staked upon the big white "O."

They paid her in notes this time, and Mrs. McMahon leant back in her chair with a gasp. "Fool! Fool that I was," she whispered, her hands clasping and unclasping themselves. "You had the money; you might have put on the maximum of nine louis, and you would have won, my dear, you would have won, and you would have won 6,300 francs—£252!"

"But, mother," Ethel whispered back, "I have won seven hundred francs already, and three hundred with the first spin, that is a thousand francs—almost my year's salary at the school!"

"You have been very fortunate" said the old lady. "And now let us go."

"Let us go, mother? No, look; they are beginning to spin again. Let me try once more?"

Mrs. McMahon gathered up the gold and crisp notes of the Bank of France and placed them in her chain purse.

"My dear," she replied, "I am almost as keen as you are to go on, but let us be content with our great good fortune. We shall have all the more money to play with when we begin upon the system to-morrow."

They vacated their seats, which were immediately occupied by people who had been standing behind them, and moved slowly through the great hall towards the doors. By this time the rooms were thronged with people of all nationalities.

The wealthiest millionaires of London, Paris and Vienna rubbed shoulders with well-dressed scoundrels known to the police of all three capitals. There was a reigning king present—a tall, elderly man with a long white beard—half the nobilities of Europe were represented. The most expensive and extravagant toilets to be found anywhere in the world at that hour were seen on either side, and yet there was a proportion of the players as poor in worldly goods as Ethel McMahon and her mother themselves; retired army men in whom the gambling fever burned and would burn until their death, young spendthrifts who had come to spend their all upon a last chance, financial defaulters who hoped by one smile of the goddess Fortune to restore money which was not theirs, and to yet preserve their honour in the eyes of the world.

And through this motley and brilliant crowd—the strangest crowd in Europe, in the strangest place—Ethel and her mother moved as if in a dream.

In the mind of the old lady a fierce and feverish greed flared like a naphtha lamp. In the mind of the girl there was but one thought, crystallised into a name—Basil! Basil! Basil!

They were near the end of the last salon and coming up to the long swing doors when Ethel started violently and half stopped.

Standing at one of the tables, within two or three yards of her, was a tall, well-built man in evening dress. His back was towards her, and there was something so absolutely familiar in the shoulders, the poise of the stranger, that she gasped.

For a moment she thought she saw Basil Gregory again—dear Basil, who was far away at the electric light works in Paris.

Then the stranger made a half turn. He was clean shaved, his complexion was swarthy, his hair was black. He was dressed also in the height of the French fashion.

No! It was not Basil, though even now there was something strangely reminiscent of her lover to the girl's eyes.

With a sigh, she passed out of the Atrium with her mother. They got their cloaks and walked slowly down the hall to the Condamine. The air was "all Arabia." A huge moon rode high in the heavens and washed the Mediterranean with silver. The flowers of the gardens sent forth an overpowering perfume—the night was sweet and dear.

"Basil! Basil! Basil!"

" ... To-morrow, my dear, we will get properly to work on the system. To-morrow!"

CHAPTER VIII

It was six o'clock on the following evening.

In a tiny room high up in the Hôtel Malmaison, above the servants' quarters, and on the roof, indeed—for the valet of Monsieur Montoyer was asthmatic and must breathe the freshest air possible—Emile Deschamps was standing.

The blinds were drawn, the room was lit by candles stuck in bottles, and presented the air more of a workshop than a bedroom.

The bed was littered with pliers, coils of insulated wire, strips of thin india-rubber, and a tube of vulcanised paste for making joints. Upon a large mahogany table close to the window stood a complicated apparatus.

At one end there was a battery of Leyden jars, then came the intricate induction coil upon a polished stand, its brass terminals glittering in the light of the candles. Beyond was the interrupter magnet and beyond that again the stout "seven-sixteens" wire which led to the electric light casing in the wall, where the hotel current had been tapped to take the place of a dynamo.

Upon that part of the table where the interrupter magnet was, there was an apparatus which in some degree resembled the keyboard of a typewriter. No letters were on these keys however. They bore numbers only, from one to thirty-six, with the addition of a nought to represent zero.

Deschamps, in list slippers, was walking nervously up and down the room. Perspiration shone upon his face. His eyes had a fixed introspective stare. He was obviously in a state of the highest possible tension.

Up and down the room he paced, like some caged animal, and every now and again he rolled a cigarette, lit it, and inhaled a few whiffs of pungent blue smoke, and threw it away. Now and then he poured himself out a cup of strong coffee from a little *cafetière* which stood upon the mantelshelf. On the hearth burned a small glowing fire of the mountain wood and fir cones which are used upon the Riviera, and beside it stood a soldering "iron" of copper, a file, and a bottle of zinc chloride solution.

Deschamps looked at his watch.

"Basil is late," he muttered to himself, mopping his brow as he did so with a very dingy handkerchief. "*Mon Dieu*, if only this were over!"

He resumed his walk, thinking deeply, checking off each incident of the great adventure, the great fight of science against the precautions and wariness of the most complete and cunning organisation in Europe.

The plans of the partners had been altered and modified. As the preparations continued in Paris and the scheme was discussed a thousand times, and with an infinity of detail which crystallised more and more into definiteness, the most important thing that was at length determined on—and the Carnet brothers had been in thorough agreement—was that play should only last for one night. The confederates had thought that phenomenal winnings, protracted over two or three days, would inevitably give rise to suspicion. These suspicions would, in all human probability, be absolutely wide of the real mark. But, at any rate, they would be certain to result in the wheel at the table where Monsieur Charles Edouard Montoyer made his colossal coups being changed for another.

It was resolved, therefore, that Basil should play, with the aid of the unseen electric influences, for one evening only. The whole thing had been worked out, and it had been found that it would be easy, if nothing went wrong, for him to win an enormous sum even within a few hours. Directly that was accomplished Deschamps would pack his apparatus and return to Paris. Basil would remain at Monte Carlo for a few days and venture a few small sums to avoid suspicion. After that he would rejoin his friend.

There was a low knock at the door, an interval of silence, and then five more distinct taps.

Deschamps knew that Basil was without, and he quietly unlocked the door and let in his friend.

Basil, tall, foreign looking, and in the most scrupulously chosen evening dress, entered the dingy little bedroom with its litter of machinery and tools. The door was locked behind him and the partners were alone together.

Deschamps started. "*Mon Dieu!*" he said, "your *sang froid* is admirable. You are—how do you call it?—cool as a cucumber. *Froid comme un concombre.* Look at me; I tremble all over, *moi!*"

Basil shrugged his shoulders. "What is the use?" he said briefly. "I have been nervous enough up to the present, but now the moment has arrived I have just *got* to keep cool. The biggest strain is on me, and if I fail now all our plans are over and it means"—he threw out his hands with a foreign gesture—"well, we won't talk of what it means."

"You are marvellous!" said the excitable little Frenchman. "You have no tremor, no compunction."

Basil shook his head. "I am strung up to go through with it," he answered, "and take what comes—fortune or prison. As for compunction, it seems to me a good deed to rob the proprietors of this hell if one can, considering all the stories I have heard during the few hours I have been here, and the evil passions I have seen displayed on all sides. And, moreover, we do it for the sake of science, to confer an inestimable benefit on the world!"

"*Bien,*" Deschamps answered. "Now, have you got the card absolutely safe? Let's compare it with mine for the last time."

From out of his pocket Basil drew an oblong slip of card. Upon it, written in a cypher invented by himself and Deschamps, in which they had perfected themselves during the last week or two, were a series of numbers. Above each number was marked the time—9:5, 9:15, etc., etc.

They went through the cards together finding them to correspond in every detail.

"And now for the watches," said Deschamps. From a kit bag in the corner of the room he produced a leather case, containing two handsome gold chronometers. "I have kept them there until now," he said, "in order that they might not become magnetised by the electric work I have been doing."

With the utmost care and nicety he adjusted the timepieces so that they did not vary, one from the other, by a single second. Then he gave one chronometer to Basil, and returned the other to the portmanteau.

"I have been playing all the day," Basil said, "with the hundred and fifty louis we reserved for that. Sometimes I lost, sometimes I won. But I spread my money about with supreme indifference. Always I put down a maximum stake, and I played upon a number. Of course, I lost many times, but I am sure I gave the desired impression to the croupiers at our table where the marked wheel is, that I was a wealthy gambler indifferent as to whether I won or lost. Towards the end I had a stroke of luck. I had put nine louis on 7, and 7 turned up. So that I won 6,300 francs. I had heard that the rule forbidding all tips to the croupiers had been recently abrogated; so that I feed the men in my neighbourhood magnificently. I shall get a seat at our table all right if I am punctual when the Casino opens for the evening play."

"And what are you going to do now?" Emile asked anxiously. "Will you stay here with me?"

"I don't think so, *mon ami*," Basil returned. "We have worked out every possible detail. The more we talk about it, the more nervous we shall become. I shall go to my room, have a little fish and a single glass of wine, and then stroll round the gardens in the fresh night air until it is time to go in." He held out his hand. "Good luck, old fellow!"

Deschamps grasped it and nodded, too full of emotion and excitement to answer.

Then Gregory quietly left the room and descended to his own.

As he walked down the passage he heard the click of the lock being shot into its place and knew that Deschamps would be alone with his machinery till midnight.

CHAPTER IX

Into the glittering rooms Basil Gregory strolled.

He had left the Hôtel Malmaison but five minutes before. The metal check for his light coat and opera hat was in his waistcoat pocket, and as he walked slowly up the Atrium, smoking a cigarette, he seemed—even in an environment where some of the most important people in the world congregate—a very distinguished person indeed.

As he came up to the doors quick-eyed officials in their black frock coats—carrion-crows people have called them—made their bows and pushed open one of the great cedar portals.

Already the word had gone round that this tall and cool gentleman was an unknown millionaire, who was pleased to amuse himself for an hour or two at the tables.

Basil entered. People were still dining. The rooms were full—they always are full—but of the ordinary and hungry crowd who do little more than venture a few francs, and hardly dare take a chair at any table when one is vacant.

Basil sauntered up to the right hand table in the large central salon. Some people call this table the "suicides' table," others give that sinister designation to another. Be that as it may, Basil found a chair and sat down—on the left of the croupier who spins the wheel and his colleague who sits behind him on a higher chair and directs the whole operations of the table.

Basil sat down, took out his watch and placed it upon the space of green baize before him. Then he drew twenty or thirty gold coins from his pocket, and a couple of five hundred franc notes.

The official who sat above the man who turned the wheel smiled down at the newcomer. It was a slack time. The table was half deserted, the rush of the diners had not yet begun.

Basil took out his cypher card and placed it carefully behind a little rampart of gold coins.

The croupier spun, and before the "*Rien ne va plus*" was uttered Basil had shoved his usual maximum of nine louis upon number 3—sitting as he did close to the wheel which divided the two long tables.

Twenty-eight turned up. Basil saw his money raked away, with the few other stakes that were adventured, with a broad smile.

No one could possibly have noticed the quick glance he gave at his watch. But that glance signified to him that for the next five minutes number "11" would be certain to win.

He put the maximum upon number 11.

He glanced again at his watch, as the croupiers began to croak their *"Faites vos jeux"* and gazed moodily round the table, which was now beginning to fill up. At that moment—a supreme moment to him—he was conscious of no particular emotion at all.

When asked about it afterwards by a certain intimate friend he always said, "Really, I felt nothing whatever."

The weary yellow-faced slave of the wheel did his duties.

All the money upon the table, at that moment, was upon even chances, upon the dozens, the *transversales*, or the columns. No single person had played direct upon a number—a thirty-five to one chance.

The big triangles of red and black at the far end of the table were both piled with gold and notes, the borders of several numbers were covered with adventurous stakes.

There was a swift "click" as the ball went home.

Number 11 had turned up.

Basil Gregory had the impulse to rise from his seat and go striding up and down those glittering halls, hugging his secret, spurning those other players who knew nothing.

Everything had occurred exactly as he had planned with Emile Deschamps. At the precise moment arranged between them the wireless message had come to the spinning ball and it had fallen, as it was directed, obedient to the unseen and unsuspected powers of science.

He drew towards him six thousand three hundred francs—two hundred and fifty two English pounds!

He looked at his watch again. The next slot in the wheel that was to be magnetised was 33. But it was not yet time. It had been arranged that he was to lose occasionally in order to divert suspicion.

He placed the maximum of nine louis upon zero. To his consternation, zero won. Again he received the enormous sum of six thousand and odd francs. He leant back in his chair, outwardly indifferent and calm, but throbbing in every nerve and pulse with wild excitement. It was true then!

A few hundred yards away, in the little bedroom on the roof, Emile Deschamps was pressing key after key with absolute precision. And as he pressed the little spinning ball, flung from the hand of the croupier, must perforce obey the invisible power that vibrated through the air.

That he had won upon zero—when he meant to lose—seemed only a minor incident in the riot of his progress.

The one man in the crowded halls of that palace—the one and only man—who could control Fortune herself, he sat there outwardly cold and impassive, while his mind and nerves were torn and wrenched as by opposing forces.

He was now more than five hundred pounds to the good, and as yet he had only played one coup of the many agreed upon by the secret code.

Already the people at the table were glancing at each other and at the impassive young man who staked a maximum each time, and had already won twice *en plein*—so unprecedented a thing to do.

He was a Russian prince, it was whispered. His French was so perfect—though it was not absolutely the French of a Frenchman—that the whispering people round the table thought he could be none other than a Russian. That he was English never occurred to anyone, for no Englishman speaks French as Basil Gregory spoke it.

The wheel was turning again, and everyone watched to see what the unperturbed figure by the croupier would do.

This time, with a glance at his cypher card, and also at his watch, Basil backed red and not a number.

Each number in the wheel has its corresponding colour, red or black, and it was as easy for him to win on an even chance as it was upon a chance of thirty-five to one. He backed red, and, far away at the top of the Hôtel Malmaison, Emile Deschamps pressed the key which magnetised the slot 18 in the wheel upon the green table—18 being a red number.

Basil placed the maximum upon red—that is, two hundred and forty pounds.

Red turned up. He had now won nearly eight hundred pounds, and round his chair were grouped a crowd of people three feet deep.

People were flocking from other tables, drawn by that nameless unknown mental telegraphy which tells the whole Casino when big wins are being made.

The whole of the great rooms became electric with an atmosphere of excitement. There was not a sound as the people thronged to Basil's table—at Monte Carlo the greatest successes, the most disastrous failures, happen in silence.

But, in that tense atmosphere, there was more than sound—there was a pressing together and focussing of human minds, converging upon one spot to witness the battle.

"Faites vos jeux, messieurs."

"Le jeu est fait."

"Rien ne va plus."

A rattle, a hushed silence—the player who had put a maximum of nine louis upon number 13 had lost!

Men and women nodded and whispered, whispered and nodded. "Monsieur's luck was about to change, *n'est-ce 'pas*?" "It is not going to be a big run after all, *hein*?"

Once more the wheel spun.

Monsieur, with extraordinary daring, placed the maximum upon 6.

Six turned up.

In front of Basil Gregory was a pile of gold, still more important and significant a bundle of crinkled blue and white notes.

He took the notes up with cool deliberation, folded many of them, and put them into the breast pocket of his coat, stretched out his hand, and put the maximum upon black.

"*Noir, dix-neuf*," the croupier croaked, and another two hundred and forty pounds was pushed over by the rakes to add to Basil's store.

By this time almost everyone at the table was playing as Basil played.

If he staked upon an 8, the number was plastered and covered with gold and notes.

Each time he won and by now a rumour of something utterly unique had spread through the whole vast building, other and lesser punters won with him. When he was up three thousand pounds against the Bank, the Bank had lost quite seventeen thousand.

The air was electric. The word had gone round. *Habitués* of the Casino crowded to watch one of those extraordinary nights of play which occur now and then—far more rarely than is supposed—and which are talked about for long afterwards. New-comers joined the throng, and still Basil Gregory sat impassive in his place, conscious that he was the centre of attention, but allowing nothing whatever to divert him from his purpose.

He glanced at his watch.

Stakes were being put upon the table timidly. The players were waiting to see what he was going to do.

He glanced at his cypher-card. The moment was marked with a tiny cross. He was now to adventure a bigger coup than ever before.

He placed the maximum of nine louis upon number 20—standing to win six thousand francs. He placed the maximum of sixty louis upon the line that covered the six figures from 16 to 21, including 20. Here also he stood to win 6,000 francs if 20 turned up.

Then he staked on black. Number 20 upon the roulette wheel is a black number, so here, again, he played the maximum and stood to win the highest possible. Finally he backed the middle dozen of the 36 numbers, here also staking the maximum of 150 louis, again making it possible to win 6,000 francs.

In that quiet place, where any outward expression of excitement or emotion is instantly suppressed, there came a low, sighing sound like the fluttering of leaves in the wind.

It was the spectators whispering to each other.

Such high play as this was beyond the experience of almost everyone. This time, getting more cautious, the other players wagered heavily against Basil. They thought such phenomenal luck as he had had could not possibly continue, and for the first time during the evening a slight sardonic smile came upon the young man's face.

He knew, they did not, with what certainty number 20 would turn up.

The wheel swung, the ball spun. "*Noir et vingt*," croaked the croupier.

And now, as the rakes pursued their remorseless way, and swept in all the stakes upon the table except Basil's maximums, there was a low murmur of surprise and consternation. Anywhere else but in the Casino it would have been a babel of tongues.

In one single minute Basil Gregory had won the huge sum of 24,000 francs—960 English pounds.

Standing by the director of the table, who sat above and behind the croupier who spun the wheel, there was now seen a tall and unobtrusive man with a pale face, a short black beard, and wearing evening dress. It was one of the heads of the permanent staff of the Administration—a mysterious being who only entered the rooms upon special occasion, a person invested with unknown powers—one of the gods!

Basil had emptied his mind of thought.

He had focussed his whole being upon what he was doing. The huge pile of wealth before him affected him no more than if the notes and gold—and by now there were many notes and but little gold—were but so many counters. Mechanically he folded bundle after bundle of thousand franc notes and placed them in the inner pocket of his coat.

And then, in the stir and rustle, he heard a sharp exclamation—unremarked by the crowd around in that moment of tension, but like an arrow through his own consciousness.

He looked up.

Opposite him, down towards the end of the table, two ladies were sitting. He had been vaguely conscious of them before, but, during all his play, he had made a point of not allowing his thoughts or glances to be distracted by the other players.

It was from one of those ladies, the young one, that he, and he alone, heard a little gasping cry.

It was the girl he loved! It was Ethel McMahon!

A mist seemed to rise up from the table as if water had been poured upon a heated plate of steel. For a moment it swayed and blotted out everything. His mind seemed to be a turning wheel. He felt little needles pricking at the back of his eyes, his blood congealed into a jelly, and the palms of his hands suddenly became covered with a film of perspiration.

Ethel!... It was Ethel! And as the mist cleared away and his mind came to attention, he knew that this was no illusion, but that in very flesh and blood Ethel and her mother were sitting almost opposite to him playing at this table, playing roulette in the world's greatest gambling hell!

The impulse to call out was almost unbearable, but he restrained it with an iron effort.

He stared hungrily at the two women, and as he did so he saw Ethel and Mrs. McMahon look up and meet his gaze. He saw this also—in their eyes was envy and consternation, but not the slightest glint of recognition.

And then he remembered his disguise—the spectacles, the shaved moustache, the foreign clothes, and swarthy complexion—and he realised that their interest in him was no more than that of any of the others.

The whole crowd, the croupiers also, were waiting to see what he would do.

The *"faites vos jeux"* was rapping out at him from all sides of the table.

He knew that he must have an instant to think or else go mad. With careless gesture he threw a couple of louis upon the table before him, not caring where they fell, and once again the wheel of chance revolved.

What did this mean? There was no answer to his agonised mental inquiry.

He saw Ethel and her mother bending over a card covered with figures—one of those system cards so frequently seen at the tables, so certain to end in disaster.

He saw also the pallor of their faces. He realised in a flash of intuition that they were losing heavily.

How to warn them, how to tell them that he and he only possessed the secret key to Fortune to-night he could not think, he could not divine.

Again he glanced at his card. Habit had become mechanical. His watch pointed to ten minutes past the hour. His directions stood clear and plain in the cypher before him.

He sorted out his notes and did what was directed.

Up there, on the top of the Hôtel Malmaison, Emile Deschamps was even at that moment pressing a certain key. The result was as inevitable as sure as Fate.

And as Fate or, rather, the cunning of science, the immense trickery of the two young geniuses, spoke, Basil saw that Ethel McMahon and her mother were very hard hit.

He watched them slant-wise from the ends of his spectacles, realising, more definitely than ever, that they were playing upon some fallacious scheme, and being sure—with a jerk of memory—that old Mrs. McMahon had unearthed one of her late husband's systems, and was pursuing it to her own ruin.

Again he won, and by now he was a rich man. The excitement was tremendous, when suddenly the tall man in evening dress announced a suspension of play.

Basil Gregory had "broken the bank."

There is a prevalent idea, among those who do not know much about Monte Carlo, that breaking the bank means that the whole play of the Casino is stopped for the night on which it occurs.

This is quite wrong.

"Breaking the bank" simply means that the resources of a particular table, out of the dozen or so tables on which roulette is played, are exhausted for a moment. In five minutes new money is brought and play goes on.

It was so now. There was a hurried consultation, and in no time lackeys were bearing oak coffers bound with brass, filled with money, to Basil's table, accompanied by three or four frock-coated officials.

The money was spread out in rows before the principal paying croupier, and six minutes had hardly passed when once more the calm, passionless voice of the director was calling upon the players to "make their game."

But in the interim, as Basil Gregory leant back in his chair, he had heard, with ears quickened by anxiety and love, these words from Ethel to her mother—words spoken in English:

"But, mother, we *cannot* go on."

Then the answer, in a sort of wail of despair: "We must go on, Ethel. This next coup is certain to put us right. We must pay no attention to the extraordinary luck of that young Russian nobleman opposite. We must adhere to your father's system. If this coup goes wrong, then we can only play twice again, and all our money will be exhausted. But I have every faith in your father's system."

Then Basil heard something about "courage," and, finally, a whispered lamentation that "our capital is so small."

Three numbers upon his cypher-card had passed by during the rebringing of money to the table.

Glancing at his watch, he saw that the time was ripe for him to play upon 16.

He was gathering up the necessary money to put upon the board, when the sallow man from the Administration pushed through the people surrounding him and whispered in his ear.

If he liked, the official did not press it at all, monsieur should have the opportunity of playing three coups against the bank. That is to say, that the ordinary maximum should be entirely abrogated in favour of monsieur, and any sum he cared to wager upon an even chance, the Administration would be pleased to meet.

The colloquy was very rapid. Deschamps had told Basil that such a thing might happen—such an offer be made to him. When a player has temporarily suspended the game at a certain table—or, in common parlance, "broken the bank"—the authorities are nearly always ready for a final sensational coup.

Basil nodded. "Certainly," he said, pulling out bundle after bundle of notes. "I will play 200,000 francs on red."

The number 16 is a red number. Basil wagered almost his whole winnings of that night without a tremor.

There was now a dead silence round the table. People clustered about it ten deep in the vain effort to see what was going on. Yet, while the wheel was turned and the ball spun, the only unconcerned person about this gigantic stake was Basil Gregory himself.

No one else put a single coin upon the table, save only a trembling old lady who sat by a young and lovely girl—an obstinate old lady, clinging to a hope.

Basil was given notes to the value of £16,000.

The most notable thing about the Casino, with its enormous resources, is the absolute impassibility of its officials.

Again Basil wagered £8,000—this time upon black.

He won, and as his money was being paid to him a loud murmur rose from the crowd—a loud murmur, broken by a sharp and pulsing cry.

A tall and beautiful girl had risen from her feet and had fallen in a deep swoon into the arms of the bystanders behind her.

There was an immediate struggle. The electric tension of the moment was over. The well-dressed crowd surged and almost fought in a panic of snapped nerves and suddenly relaxed excitement.

People came surging from all sides. The other tables were deserted, and, far away through the great halls, those who were playing *trente-et-quarante* rose from their cards with listening ears.

In that supreme moment Basil Gregory did not lose his head. He gathered up his enormous winnings. The pockets of his coat bulged with wealth. And Ethel McMahon was being carried out into the Atrium, followed by her mother in a state of wild hysteria, before he rose from his seat.

He took six thousand-franc notes from one of his pockets. To each of the six croupiers he gave a note.

Then he sauntered quietly out into the huge hall.

Under the brilliant electric lights which gleamed upon the marble he saw little groups of people—each group seeming quite small in the immensity—talking earnestly together.

As he came out among them every head was turned, though of Ethel and her mother he saw not a trace.

But as he went to the cloak-room, and delivered his metal ticket, two or three commissionaires came up to him with awed and respectful faces.

"That young lady?" he said, "and the elder one with her?"

"It was nothing, monsieur," one of the men hastened to say. "They are two English ladies staying at the *pension* in the Rue Grimaldi. Your success, monsieur, unnerved them. They have been sent home in a *voiture*."

Basil nodded as he was helped into his long, dark coat.

With a smile he distributed a few gold coins, and then, alone, unattended, he walked out into the warm, aromatic night, and strolled to his adjacent hotel among flower-bordered paths, under the twin lights of electricity and the great, red moon of the South.

At the Hôtel de Paris, at the Métropole, at Ciro's, people were gathering for gay supper parties.

As he entered the huge, brilliantly decorated lounge of the Malmaison, groups of wealthy people were smoking a preliminary cigarette before supper. Some of them—many of them—recognised him, and nodded and whispered to each other, but he entered the lift and went straight to his own room.

He turned up the electric lights, and locked the door. And then, from pocket and pocket, he poured out crackling, crumpled heaps of notes, heavy handfuls of gold—the wealth of which he had dreamed.

After a minute or two, without even locking the door of his sitting-room, he stumbled out of it and up the stairs to the servants' quarters.

He gave the signal knocks.

He was at once admitted to the dingy little bedroom-workshop.

Emile Deschamps was there. The Frenchman's face was as grey as evening ice.

He was staring at his apparatus in a sort of stupor, and by his side the chronometer ticked.

Emile gave a loud shout as Basil tumbled into the place.

"It is done, then?" he gasped. "*Mon ami*, it is a thing done?"

All grimy as he was Basil led his friend down into his sitting-room.

* * * * *

At two o'clock on the afternoon of the next day two English ladies, accompanied by a little, swarthy Frenchman, with a dressing-case which never left his hands, rolled out of the station of Monte Carlo, *en route* for Paris.

For two days after this Monsieur Montoyer was observed to walk distractedly through the salons and occasionally to place a maximum upon a single number. Monsieur Montoyer did not repeat his successes, and those who followed his play cursed him and their own credulity deeply and silently.

The great night when Fortune smiled upon the "young Russian nobleman" is still remembered by the assiduous acolytes of Chance. It is talked about, and given as an instance to new-comers of what bold, indifferent play can accomplish.

Nobody connects Sir Basil Gregory, Bart., the head of the great firm of Deschamps, Gregory and Co., which has revolutionised wireless telegraphy, with the spectacled, clean-shaven young gentleman who made such a sensation one night in the Casino at Monte Carlo.

Sir Basil and Lady Gregory spend almost all their days in the charming old house they have bought near Falmouth.

But on the Riviera there is an old, old lady—the well-known Madame McMahon—who still haunts the gambling hells of the Continent. She is a recognised figure. She has a marvellous system which never comes off, but when she gets into difficulties with the proprietors of her *pension,* mysterious telegraphic drafts upon the local bank always arrive in the nick of time, either from Cornwall or from Quimperlé, in Brittany, where Monsieur Edouard and Monsieur Charles Carnet have a house, and are churchwardens of the unique cathedral.

THE END.

Lector House believes that a society develops through a two-fold approach of continuous learning and adaptation, which is derived from the study of classic literary works spread across the historic timeline of literature records. Therefore, we aim at reviving, repairing and redeveloping all those inaccessible or damaged but historically as well as culturally important literature across subjects so that the future generations may have an opportunity to study and learn from past works to embark upon a journey of creating a better future.

This book is a result of an effort made by Lector House towards making a contribution to the preservation and repair of original ancient works which might hold historical significance to the approach of continuous learning across subjects.

HAPPY READING & LEARNING!

LECTOR HOUSE

LECTOR HOUSE LLP
E-MAIL: info@lectorhouse.com

9 789356 146853

Printed by Libri Plureos GmbH in Hamburg,
Germany

9 789356 146853